For more than forty years,
Yearling has been the leading name
in classic and award-winning literature
for young readers.

Yearling books feature children's
favorite authors and characters,
providing dynamic stories of adventure,
humor, history, mystery, and fantasy.

Trust Yearling paperbacks to entertain,
inspire, and promote the love of reading
in all children.

Praise for **With Love from Spain, Melanie Martin:**

"Carol Weston gets girls. The author of *With Love from Spain, Melanie Martin*, the latest in her globetrotting series, has a loyal fan base that *sooo* relates to Mel, an 11-year-old with an annoying little brother." —*Parenting*

"Another thoroughly enjoyable adventure...delightful...lively...Weston does a great job of giving Melanie an authentic preteen voice....Her greatest feat, however, is expertly weaving loads of history and art, as well as Spanish words (with pronunciations), throughout the text." —*Booklist*

"Appealing young heroine." —*Vanity Fair*

"Funny and entertaining." —*Toronto Sun*

"A great children's book." —*New York Daily News*

"When Melanie and her family go to Spain . . . Melanie's trip fills her diary with Spanish words, Spanish customs, museums and—best of all—Spanish romance!" —*Boston Herald*

"Weston's not just any teen-lit writer—she's also the reigning columnist for *GL Magazine*." —*Newsweek*

OTHER YEARLING BOOKS YOU WILL ENJOY

WITH LOVE FROM SPAIN, MELANIE MARTIN, *Carol Weston*

MELANIE MARTIN GOES DUTCH, *Carol Weston*

THE DIARY OF MELANIE MARTIN, *Carol Weston*

VOYAGE OF ICE, *Michele Torrey*

SWEAR TO HOWDY, *Wendelin Van Draanen*

GIFTS FROM THE SEA, *Natalie Kinsey-Warnock*

THE TRIAL, *Jen Bryant*

THE LEGACY OF GLORIA RUSSELL, *Sheri Gilbert*

THE WICKED, WICKED LADIES IN THE HAUNTED HOUSE
Mary Chase

to Becca—
Enjoy!

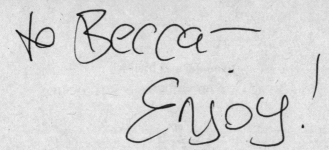

Melanie in Manhattan

BY
CAROL WESTON

Carol Weston (signature)

A YEARLING BOOK

to emme and lizzi—
my city girls

Published by Yearling, an imprint of Random House Children's Books
a division of Random House, Inc., New York

Visit us on the Web! www.randomhouse.com/kids

Educators and librarians, for a variety of teaching tools, visit us at
www.randomhouse.com/teachers

ISBN-13: 978-0-440-42040-8
ISBN-10: 0-440-42040-7

Reprinted by arrangement with Alfred A. Knopf Books for Young Readers

Printed in the United States of America

July 2006

10 9 8 7 6 5 4 3 2 1

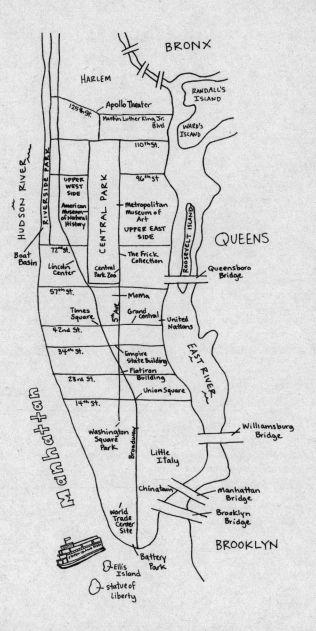

March 31

Dear Brand-New Diary,

WHOA! I can't believe my eyes!!! 👀

I am about to be face to face (or girl to statue) with the Statue of Liberty!!

I LOVE the Statue of Liberty!!! She is green from her spiky crown to her big flip-flops, and she's draped in a toga dress that makes her look like a Roman goddess—an American Roman goddess.

We're on a boat because Dad's boss invited us to a party. The invitation said, "Don't be late—the boat won't wait!"

The bad thing is that there are no kids my age. The worse thing is that my brother, Matt the Brat, is acting *his* age—seven.

1

He keeps waving at other boats and shouting "Ahoy!" He's even ahoying seagulls. And there are *lots* of seagulls. ⌢ ⌣⌢

I told him to quit it, but he said, "Ahoy!"

I said, "I hope a seagull poops on you!"

He said, "Ahoy!" again.

There is nothing more annoying
than a brother who's ahoying!

Seriously! You'd think Matt would look up at the Statue of Liberty. She is getting closer and cl0sER and bigger and bigger!

How can he be so clueless? How can he not see what's right in front of him??

twenty minutes later

I couldn't take it anymore, so finally I said, "Hey, Ahoy Boy! Look over there!"

He looked, and instead of saying, "Ahoy!" he said, "Awesome!"

The Statue of Liberty is pretty, but not pretty-pretty. More like: proud. But not show-offy proud. Dignified proud. As though she knows she's done the exact right thing, welcoming new people to America.

It feels like she is even welcoming us back home from our trip to Spain.

Dad came over and took pictures of me sticking up one hand and holding my diary (you) in the other: The Statue of Melanie!

Matt asked, "Can *we* have a party on a boat someday?"

Dad said, "Don't hold your breath!" So of course Matt started holding his breath—and making a big deal of it. Dad told us that the Statue of Liberty was built by two French guys: Eiffel (who designed the Eiffel Tower) and Bartholdi (who made her look like his mom). Dad also said that her nose is four-and-a-half feet long. I doubt mine is even two inches!

We were getting really close to the Statue of Liberty, and I couldn't stop staring. It was like I was under a spell—a spell Moron Matt kept trying to break! His freckly cheeks were puffed out and his blue eyes were wide open and he kept shifting from one foot to the other. Finally he exhaled and asked, "Think she could catch a fly ball?"

I said, "No! She would never put her torch down."

"Think she's ticklish under her arm?"

"Ha ha. You're hilarious."

"Think she has B.O. and needs a de-ODOR-ant?"

"Matt, you immature idiot, stop trying to be funny."

"I'm funny *without* trying."

"No, you are so *not* funny, it's not even funny. Besides, there are some things you just don't joke about."

"Like what?"

"Like the Statue of Liberty. Duh! Leave her alone!"

Matt shrugged, then he and Dad left me alone. Alone with the most famous statue in America!

Seagulls are squawking and grown-ups are talking, but Lady Liberty is serious, strong, and still. (That's an alliteration.)

And sure of herself. She is the *opposite* of moody!

What would it feel like to be the Statue of Liberty: to be so solid and so permanent?

She is now getting farther and farther and smaller and smaller. . . .

We passed by Ellis Island (where immigrants used to arrive) and are heading toward Lower Manhattan (where the twin towers used to be). Mom came to check on me, but since I was writing, she just put her hands on the railing. I can always tell when she is thinking about the towers because she gets extra quiet.

A long time ago, before security people started looking at everyone's shoes at airports, America tried to put out a great big welcome mat for anyone who wanted to come here.

Then things got more complicated.

I'm lucky. I've traveled pretty much and I'm learning about the world. For some reason, though, I don't usually think about being American.

Right now, what I'm thinking is that if I had a flaming torch, I would hold it high and shine it back at the Statue of Liberty. But I really wish I had a *magic* torch—a torch that could stop time in its tracks! Why? Because I like being in fifth grade and having a best friend (Cecily) and a boy I like (Miguel). I like things exactly the way they are. Life feels . . .

Almost perfect,
Melanie in Manhattan

P.S. It's a good thing I put you in my backpack. Normally I keep travel diaries—which I did in Italy, Holland, and Spain. This will be my very first Melanie At Home diary!

April Fool's Day
Sunday morning

Dear Diary,

It's April Fool's, but I swear I'm not making this up.

Over spring break, while I was off in Spain having my first kiss with Miguel, our mice, Milkshake and Pancake, were here having a whole entire family!

They multiplied!

We didn't even know they were pregnant!

We didn't even know they were a boy and a girl.

Now instead of two, there are ten!

The babies are red, blind, bald, teeny tiny, and somewhere in between cute and disgusting. (To be honest, they are more on the disgusting side.)

They keep hanging on to the mother to nurse. Poor Milkshake! She must be exhausted. You know the song "Three Blind Mice"? Well, she has *eight* blind mice.

Pancake is already trying to make more babies (if you know what I mean). It's like a TV nature show.

In the world, mice get eaten up by cats and owls and other predators, so Mother Nature has to make sure that each mouse pair makes tons of babies so that a few can survive to make tons more babies. In Matt's room, however, there are no predators. (Matt can be an Annoying Little Brother, or A.L.B., but at least he doesn't eat mice.)

What are baby mice called anyway? Baby dogs are puppies; baby cats are kittens; baby owls are owlets; baby ducks are ducklings. But baby mice aren't micies or micetens or micelets or mouselings.

Whatever they're called, Matt is excited about them. He said:

It's kind of nice
to have ten mice.

Mom and Dad are not excited. They are the opposite. Me, I'm . . .

In between,

Mouse Owner Mel

Dear Diary,

"It was on the *forehead*?!" That's what Suze asked when I told her about my first kiss. I would never have told her at all—except she came over with Cecily, and I was dying to show my best friend the vacation scrapbook I'd just made.

Suze is new. She joined our class in September. Her real name is Susan, but everyone calls her Suze (rhymes with Ooze). She's always talking about how popular she was in her old school and blah blah blah. I guess she's already kind of popular in our school too.

"It's not like Miguel and I were alone," I explained. "We were in an airport."

"I still don't get it," Suze said. "He's your mom's old boyfriend's son and he lives in Spain??"

I said yes and showed the photos of the bullfight, gypsy dancers, and my favorites, the ones of Miguel and me at the castle. I'd already put one photo in a heart-shaped frame on my dresser. My hair is blowing all over the place, and my eyes look really happy.

8

"Think he's cute?" I asked.

"¡Sí!" Cecily nodded. "You two make a cute couple."

"He has the best smile," I said, and that got *me* smiling.

"Too bad it wasn't a lips kiss," Suze said. "They're better!" She laughed like a hyena, and I sat there like an April Fool.

"Have you talked to him?" Cecily asked.

"My parents won't let me. It's too expensive, and Spain is in a different time zone."

"So you and your boyfriend are e-mailing?" Suze asked.

I'd never actually called Miguel my boyfriend, but I liked the way it sounded, and I liked our first kiss, so I said, "I've sent three short e-mails—one for each day since we got home."

Suze raised one eyebrow. "He hasn't answered?"

I shook my head.

Cecily said, "He will." To Suze, she added, "Look at this photo of Columbus's tomb."

"Omigod! Last week we were shopping at Columbus Circle," Suze said. "And Cecily pointed out the statue of Columbus and told me you were in Spain."

Well, it didn't make me feel good that Cecily was thinking about me. It made me feel bad that she was shopping with Suze. I'd been away less than two weeks and Suze had jumped right in.

"We got lip gloss," Cecily said.

"And bras!" Suze added, then pulled her shirt off her shoulder to reveal a slim lavender strap.

"I'm wearing mine too!" Cecily yanked out a matching strap.

"Cute cute cute!" I said. But I was thinking, "Puke puke puke."

Two comments:

1. I wish Suze weren't oozing all over my friendship with Cecily.

2. I wish *I* needed a bra.

Bralessly,
Melanie

P.S. Most kids in my grade are NOT wearing bras, but Cecily started wearing one when she turned eleven on Halloween, and Suze came to school with one on!

4/2 after dinner
In Dad's BIG Chair

Dear Diary,

Dad and Mom were looking at the boat party photos.

"I love this!" Mom said. "Lady Melanie carrying a torch. You know that expression, don't you?"

"Sounds familiar . . ."

"When you're carrying a torch for someone," Dad explained, "you care a lot about that person—even if you're not together anymore."

Matt said, "You mean like Mom cared about her old Spanish boyfriend?" During vacation, Mom *admitted* that even though she's happily married to Dad, her exbf would always be important to her. Which may be legal and normal and allowed. But it's still surprising coming from a mom.

"Not exactly, Matt." Mom laughed. "When someone is carrying a torch, that person is thinking *too much* about the past. He or she may even be lighting the way for the long-lost love to return."

Matt started wadding up pages from the Sunday *New York Times* and tossing them into our living room

11

trash can. "Hey, Melanie, want to play Apartment Basketball?"

"Matt, I'm eleven."

"Do you, Dad?"

"Sure."

Matt turned to me and said, "Score!"

But I was still thinking about torches. Am I carrying a torch for Miguel? I decided not to write him today.

Yours with a torch,
Lady Mel

4/4 at 4!
after school

Dear Diary,

This morning the fifth-grade Spanish classes all went on a field trip to the Hispanic Society of America. Guess who organized it? Mom!

Mom was a little nervous, but I was more nervous. It's embarrassing having Mom stand in front of everyone acting like a teacher. I know she's not acting—she *is* an art teacher. But still!

Mom showed us Spanish paintings, starting with *Holy Family* by El Greco. Christopher said, "Baby Jesus looks like an old man!" Mom said it took painters a long time to realize that it was okay to paint Jesus as a regular roly-poly baby. Christopher whispered, "Check out His teeny tiny you-know-what." Suze cracked up, Mom ignored them both, and I wondered how I could have ever liked Christopher.

Mom asked what we thought of a close-up by Velázquez of a serious, dark-haired girl with a sweet almost-smile. The girl looks half innocent, half wise. This boy named Justin raised his hand and said she looked like me—but with brown eyes! Everyone laughed, and I tried not to blush—which probably backfired and made me blush extra.

We tromped downstairs, and Mom said she wanted us to see the "real jewel" of the collection. I thought "real jewel" sounded real dorky, but no one else noticed.

The "jewel" was a portrait of a proud duchess, a widow. She is a funny-looking Spanish lady with big black eyebrows and black hair under a poofy black veil. She's wearing a long fancy skirt. Mom asked, "What is she doing?"

Christopher said, "Pointing down," then pointed to her pointer finger. He almost touched the painting— and Mom almost had a heart attack!

Mom told *him* to move back and told *us* to look at the lady's two rings. In tiny shiny letters, one said her name, Alba, and the other said another name. "Who can read it?"

Cecily raised her hand. "Goya!"

"Yes! And on the sand," Mom said, "it says 'Sólo Goya' or 'Only Goya' in big loopy letters. She is announcing to the whole wide world that her heart belongs to one man, Francisco Goya, whose name appears at her feet. She's expressing her love and loyalty, and by painting her, Goya is expressing his devotion too. His *devoción*" (Day Vo Syon).

On the bus ride back, Suze and I both wanted to sit with Cecily. So we all three ended up sitting together on the very last seat. Cecily said she was glad my mom arranged the trip because she liked it, and she'd never even heard of that museum.

"Really?" Suze said. "No offense"—I could already feel myself getting offended—"but I think museum trips are boring. My old school had a whale-watching trip."

Cecily turned to me and whispered, "Any e-mails yet?"

15

"Not yet."

"Don't worry."

"I'm not. I'm being patient." And it's true. When I think about Miguel, I don't worry. It mostly feels like a wonderful secret, sweet and warm.

Suze had been folding and writing on a square of paper. She put it on her thumbs and fingertips and smushed it together, apart, together, apart. Then she made Cecily and me pick colors and numbers and told our fortunes.

Cecily's was: "Friendships can change."

I hope not!

Mine was: "Someone has a crush on you."

I hope so!

Patiently,

Mellie

I've been working on this poem:

> If an artist painted me,
> What would the artist see?
> A loyal girl who is sometimes shy?
> A girl who likes a faraway guy?
> Would it say "Miguel" on my hand?
> Or "Only Miguel" on the sand?

April 5
afternoon

Dear Diary,

I can't believe I signed off "Patiently" yesterday because today I am officially impatient!

I also can't believe I thought things felt almost perfect last week because now things feel totally imperfect!

I called Cecily, and her mom said she was out with "Susan." I felt like saying, "You mean Suze the Ooze," but said, "Thank you, Priscilla. No message."

Whenever I check my e-mail (which, I confess, is a

17

little too often), I look for Miguel's e-mail address. But it's never there. The little voice says, "You've Got Mail," but it's not the mail I want.

Since there is never any New Mail from Miguel, I've been opening my Sent Mail and rereading what I wrote him.

Pathetic, right?

I just want to be sure I haven't sent anything stupid or cheesy or boring that I should have deleted.

Here are the three e-mails I've sent so far:

E-mail #1:

> *Hola* Miguel—
> It's me, Melanie!! We're back in New York and I'm jet-lagged. I hope this e-mail reaches you. Right now you are probably asleep because it's dinnertime here. I hope you are having a nice dream!
> *Adiós,*
> Melanie

When I sent that, it seemed like a friendly e-mail. Now I'm wondering if it was weird that I said I hoped he was having a nice dream. Was that too personal? Then again, it's not like I said, "a nice dream about me," or anything! It wasn't thaaat inappropriate, I don't think. But what do I know? I'm not used to writing boys!

E-mail #2:

Hi Miguel,

¿*Cómo estás?* I am fine. Please write me because I am really hoping to hear from you. It is good to be back home but I like vacation better. My door-man friend, Gustavo, said I learned a lot of Spanish. I told him I had a good teacher! :)

Yours,

Melanie

P.S. Matt says *hola*.

I think that one's okay, but maybe not. When I wrote I was "really" hoping to hear from him, did it sound desperate, like I have no life unless he e-mails? And did it sound like I'm showing off about my Spanish?? Was it dumb to write "Yours" at the end? No, I think it's okay. I just wish I *knew* it was okay.

E-mail #3 (this is the one that worries me the most):

```
Dear Miguel,
Yesterday we went on a boat trip.
You would have loved it. We saw the
Statue of Liberty. France gave it to
us in 1886. Spain is full of things
that are thousands of years old, but
to us in America, 1886 seems like a
long time ago.
To me in New York, even a few days
seems like a long time ago.
Are you there, Miguel???
miss u,
Melanie
```

Why did I ask if he was there? And why did I write "miss u"? Does "miss u" sound mushy? Will he even get that u = you, or will he think I can't spell? I bet he will get it—but what will he think of it?

I wish I could press Unsend, but we're on different systems.

I wish he'd write!!!

Once you send an e-mail, you want one back. You can't help it. So I feel as if I've shouted "Hello" three times into one of those echo-y archways in Central Park, and instead of hearing Hello Hellooo Hellooooooooo, all I'm hearing is . . . nothing nothing nothing.

Sometimes I think I must have made the whole thing up.

Then I look at the photos I put in my scrapbook, and touch the silver fan necklace he put around my neck, and leaf through my travel diary, and I know Miguel is real, even if he is far away and silent.

This isn't all in my head, because it was in his head too.

Maybe since I like to write (I'm *always* writing), it's

easier for me to e-mail him than it is for him to e-mail me. But he could still send a short paragraph. Or a sentence. Or a word! Or a smiley!!

In my diary, I'm tempted to scribble: I hate love.

But I don't.

L❤ve,
Melanie
P.S.

I'm just a female
who wants an e-mail!

an hour later

Dear Diary,

I have been staring at my computer screen, trying to make Miguel write me. But he hasn't. So for better or worse, I just wrote him again. Even if it is his turn.

And I didn't press Send Later or Delete. I pressed Send.

I hope he doesn't think I'm a stalker.

Here it is, my fourth and final e-mail:

Dear Miguel,

I was thinking of you and of Blanquito, your grandmother's bird. Remember when I told you that we had two pet
mice? When we were on vacation, they
had babies! Eight babies! Their ears
have opened but their eyes haven't.
They are growing fur and whiskers and
getting cuter by the day.

Yesterday my mother took my Spanish
class to see paintings by Velázquez and
Goya. It reminded me of when you and I
went to the museum in Madrid.

I don't know if you are getting my
e-mails, but I want you to know that
I've been wearing my necklace.

Gracias again for it.

Melanie

I could probably analyze that one for hours, as
though it were a tricky paragraph we're studying in
English. But I'm not going to let myself. Not today

anyway! Besides, all I'm trying to say is: Write back!!!

Wishingly,
May Lahnee (as Miguel used to call me!)

P.S. I made sure I have Miguel's correct address. I do.

April 9
bedtime,

Dear Diary,

In Spanish today, Señora Barrios asked me to describe a friend, so I said that Cecily is my best friend or *mejor amiga* (May Hhhor Ah Me Ga), and that she's nice or *simpática* (Seem Pa Teek Ah), and that she has a bunny and a cat—*un conejo* (Oon Co Nay Hhho) and *un gato* (Oon Ga Toe).

I wish I could really speak Spanish because I wanted to say more about Cecily's cat. Like when Cheshire licks himself, the tip of his little tongue sometimes gets stuck outside his mouth, and it looks so so so cute. And when he was a kitten, he used to run up to mirrors and pounce at himself, but now that he's older, when he tries to jump on Cecily's bed, he sometimes misses and goes tumbling off, and then makes it on the second try, and it's sort of funny but also sort of sad.

Of course, I didn't know how to say any of that in Spanish.

After class, Justin, this boy I've never really noticed much, said he was amazed by how much Spanish I'd learned over spring break. I said I learned *un poco* (Oon Poe Coe) or a little, but that my Spanish still wasn't *bueno* (Bway No) or good.

He said, "Sounds *bueno* to me."

I said, "Your best subject is math, right?" (Maybe I have noticed him a little.)

"I like math."

"Even word problems?"

"Especially word problems." He laughed and looked into my eyes. His are pale green with brown flecks.

Well, just now when I was checking my e-mail (and rereading—or re-rereading—my old letters), I got an instant message from justjustin. I guessed justjustin might be Justin, so I accepted the IM and he wrote **hi** so I wrote hi and he wrote **sup** and I wrote nm (for not much) and he wrote **if u ever need help in math just ask** so I wrote k and he wrote **k** and I wrote thnx and he typed **g2g** (for got to go) so I typed cu and that was that.

g2g,
MM

the tenth of *abril* (Ah Breel),
which means April

Dear Diary,

Mom and Dad's passports were about to expire, so they got their photos taken today and were in the kitchen filling out applications for new passports. Matt took a peek and said, "*That's* Dad's new passport photo?!"

Mom said, "Dad's handsome but not photogenic."

Dad corrected, "Mom's kind but Dad's old."

"You are not old!" Mom said. "You just should have shaved. And opened your eyes a little more."

I examined Dad's new photo, and well, it does stink. I said, "At least yours is good, Mom."

Matt said, "Dad's looks like a police picture of a bad guy."

"A mug shot!" I agreed.

"C'mon, kids, a little respect," Mom said. "You're talking about my distinguished husband."

"The decrepit almost-forty-year-old," Dad said.

"Forty is not old," Mom said.

"It's not young," Matt argued. Mom frowned at him, so he added, "But it's not decrepit either—whatever that means."

"Old," Dad explained. "Worn out. Broken down. Ancient."

"Enough!" Mom said, and kissed Dad. To be honest, she seemed a teeny bit worried, like when she checks our foreheads to see if we have a fever.

Observantly,
Mel

before school

Dear Diary,

Mice are more fun to watch than television! My favorite thing is when two mice get on the treadmill and spin each other around and take turns holding on upside down. It's like a mouse Ferris wheel. Matt's favorite thing is taking the mice on one-at-a-time field trips in his pocket around the apartment.

I like our mouse family, but when the pet store man sold us a pair and said they were female, he really should have checked to make sure.

Mom says life is full of surprises—but I like when life's more predictable! I *don't* like that everything is changing, from my pet mice to my best friend!

Two questions:

1. If I saw a mouse in the basement of our building, would I still be scared?

2. How come mice are cute but rats are disgusting?

> We started with a single pair
> And now have fuzz balls everywhere.

Fuzzily,
Mel Belle

April 11

Dear Diary,

I'm glad you're not mad at me, because everyone else is! I forgot to take something out of my pocket, and it ruined all the laundry.

It was makeup. Cecily gave me concealer, which is beige stuff you put on your face to hide zits. I don't even have zits yet. I put it in my pocket and forgot about it. Well, the container opened up in the washing machine and went round and round, and the beige stuff got all over *everything*. Matt's T-shirts and Dad's boxers and Mom's gym socks.

It's like the clothes have zits!

I wanted to make a joke about our laundry being full of surprises, but since Mom was mad, I just said, "Sorry," which usually works.

Not this time. Instead of saying, "It's okay, Tootsie Roll, I know it was an accident," Mom sighed and said it's enough to wash, dry, and fold clothes, she should *not* be expected to check everybody's pockets for keychains-gum-quarters-rings-marbles-feathers-pebbles-erasers-Chap Stick-and-makeup. She said emptying pockets was *our* job, not hers. She added that we were getting older, and she also didn't like that when we tried on lots of shirts and chose one, we stuffed the rejects in the hamper instead of putting them back on the shelf where they belonged.

I was about to point out that I never put *feathers* in my pocket—that was Matt—and that I hadn't put any clean clothes in the hamper since last week. But

I decided just to mumble "Sorry" again.

Mom held up a pair of little boy underpants with beige polka dots and said, "Apology accepted, but Melanie, this was not your 'finest hour.'"

Which got me wondering. When was my "finest hour"? Did I miss it? Was I even paying attention? Did it happen over spring break with Miguel? Do I have any more ahead?

YOUR UNFINE FRIEND,

Messy MEL

P.S. The concealer got ruined too.

bedtime

Dear Diary,

I keep turning my computer on then off, and there are never any messages. Which makes me want to say, "Okay, okay, okay! I get the message!"

Would my English teacher call that "irony"?

Ironically,

Mel

P.S. I can't believe I referred to Miguel as my boyfriend. He's not even my pen pal!

P.P.S. At least I never expected Miguel to call. If I'd gotten hopeful every time the phone rang, I'd feel worse than I already do.

April 13

Dear Diary,

Friday the 13th is usually an unlucky day, but today I turned on my computer oh-so-casually, and my heart started pounding because there was an e-mail from Miguel! My mouth got dry and my stomach flipped over, and I was afraid to click on his name but too excited not to.

Here's what he wrote:

MELANIE:

FOUR E-MAILS! THIS IS VERY GREAT! IT IS LIKE RECEIVING MANY PRESENTS WHEN IT IS NOT MY BIRTHDAY!

I AM SORRY I DID NOT WRITE, BUT I HAVE BEEN AWAY ON

EASTER HOLIDAY WITH MY MOTHER (MY PARENTS ARE STILL SEPARATE). I AM NOW AT THE OFFICE OF MY FATHER. HE SENDS GREETINGS.

THE MOUSES SOUND CUTE. BUT I HAVE TO TELL YOU ABOUT BLANQUITO. SHE FLEW INTO MY GRANDMOTHER'S DISH-WASHER. MY GRANDMOTHER DID NOT KNOW THIS AND SHE TURNED ON THE WASHER WITH THE BIRD INSIDE. AT THE END, IT WAS DEAD. (CLEAN BUT DEAD.) WE WERE ALL VERY SAD BE-CAUSE BLANQUITO WAS A SWEET LITTLE BIRD.

FORGIVE ME FOR NOT TO WRITE SOONER. WILL YOU? I WANT TO KNOW HOW ARE YOU. EVEN THOUGH YOU ARE ACROSS THE ATLANTIC, YOU ARE HERE IN MY THOUGHTS.

UN BESITO,

MIGUEL

Beso (Bay So) is the word for kiss, so besito (Bay Sea Toe) must mean little kiss.

Well, a little kiss is A BIG DEAL!

It was weird. I was all alone in my room with the door closed, but it was as though Miguel were right in front of me. I mean, I was looking at the screen, feeling warm and happy and tingly and melty, and my

33

heart was beating fast and my face was tilted to the side. And I was smiling because even though Miguel is far away, he suddenly felt very close.

I almost gave the computer a *beso*. Instead, I wrote back:

```
Dear Miguel,
   Gracias for your e-mail. Where did
you go on vacation?
   I am very sorry to hear about Blanquito.
I bet your grandmother misses him. :-(
   Our baby mice are now a little over
two weeks old and their eyes just
opened. Soft fur and open eyes do a lot
for a mouse's appearance! The babies
are busy busy busy exploring their nest
of wood shavings and cotton balls.
   I wish you could see them!
   Hasta la próxima,
   Melanie
```

After I wrote, "I wish you could see them," I tried to

get myself to write, "And I wish I could see you," but I couldn't. I also tried to get myself to sign off with *un besito*, but I couldn't do that either. Thing is, I didn't want to write "Love" or "Sincerely" or "Bye" or "Your friend" or "XOXO" either.

It took me over half an hour to come up with *Hasta la próxima* (Ah Sta La Proke C Ma). It means "Until next time" and it's what Miguel and I said to each other at the airport in Spain when I told him that I didn't want to say goodbye or *adiós*.

Hasta la próxima,
Mellie

P.S. I IMed Cecily Guess who wrote me? and she IMed back MIGUEL? and I IMed back :) :) :) and then she IMed omg for omigod and then she phoned.

Dear Diary,

When Matt and I fed the mouse babies today, we were in for a surprise. It was as if the babies had all gone crazy—at the exact same time.

They were leaping like grasshoppers or frogs or popcorn! Matt opened the top of their cage so we could feed them berries, and the babies sprang straight up.

At first it was scary, then weird, then funny. Matt looked in one of his science books and we found out that at about sixteen days, if baby mice are disturbed, they jump straight in the air to avoid danger.

Well, obviously the pet store man should have checked the mice's private parts and also warned us about the Bouncing Baby Stage!

Matt and I named the mice: Leap Frog, Pirate, Buccaneer, Ahoy, Stuart Little, Happy, Mickey, and MouseMouse. (Matt chose MouseMouse in honor of DogDog.)

Uh-oh. Matt needs me. He's by himself with the jumping micelets!

Jumpily,

Melanie Martin, Mouse Expert

P.S.

I Like hearing from Miguel;
I Like knowing all is well.
I'm sure that he will write again,
but it would help if I knew when.

April 16
bedtime

Dear Diary,

Tomorrow is our math-class field trip to Lincoln Center. We sometimes go there for operas, plays, ballet, or jazz—but not math. Mom loves the giant Marc Chagall murals in the Metropolitan Opera House.

I laid out my clothes, then changed my mind four times, which is two times more than usual, which sounds like the beginning of a word problem.

It's **Hard** to choose what to wear,
but how come I even care ?

Night!
Mel

P.S. I stuffed the three reject outfits in the hamper, then got them out and put them neatly back on my shelf.

April 17

Dear Diary,

Field trips used to be so much fun. This one should have been . . . and almost was.

I remember my first field trip ever, back in kindergarten. We all piled into a big yellow bus and rumbled up to an orchard. I'd just met Cecily (she was missing her two front teeth), and we sat next to each other.

If it's possible to look back and point to a day when two people became best friends, that was the day for us.

Sunshine poured everywhere, and the second we got

38

off the bus, we smelled the apples, tart and sweet. Teachers gave us bags with handles, and we were supposed to fill the bags to the top.

Cecily filled hers in a minute. Ripe red apples seemed to pop off their stems. Maybe I was trying too hard, because every time I saw an apple I liked, I had to climb up high or reach in deep or twist or pull or yank, and I almost got stung by two different bees.

When I finally filled my bag, Cecily said, "Let's have lunch." But I'd left my lunch on the bus! She said, "Don't worry," opened her brown bag, handed me half her banana-and-jelly sandwich, and we've been friends ever since.

Back at school that day, we counted and weighed our apples and cut them into halves and quarters. To the teachers, it was beginner math. To us, it was Fun With Apples.

Well, today our teacher, Ms. Riley, broke us into groups. Mine was Norbert, Cecily, Justin, and me. Perfect! I like Ms. Riley, but at the last minute, for no good reason, she made a switch. She put Suze in our group and plunked me in a different group. It was so not fair!

Each group got a ruler, a calculator, and a two-foot piece of string. With that and our "eyes and brains," we were supposed to figure out how many gallons of water fit in the well of the cool central fountain and how many square tiles are in the reflecting pool in front of the Vivian Beaumont Theater and stuff about the angles of a spindly steel sculpture by Alexander Calder.

Since Justin is way better at math than anyone in my group, I asked him for help. Twice. He's really nice. And smart but not conceited. He's like a teacher: He doesn't just give out answers; he explains how to get them.

He even knows the long number for pi.

I think of pi as 3.14. But he knows the first fifteen numbers of it by heart! It's 3.14159 . . . oops, that's all I know.

He said his mom is a math teacher and that his family calls March 14 "Pi Day." Every 3/14, they bake a pie. If it's a weekend, they say "Happy Pi Day" and eat it at exactly 1:59. Justin said, "It might sound dumb, but my sister Katie and I look forward to March 14. It's like having a whole extra holiday."

I said it didn't sound dumb and asked what kind of pie they made last month. He said apple. The sun was shining softly on his face, and his sandy hair matched his eyes. Maybe his eyes are more hazel than pale green. Cecily and I became friends during a field trip, and I was thinking maybe Justin and I were becoming friends too.

"Omigod!" Suze suddenly butted in. "Lincoln Center! I just realized: Last time I was here, it was for the Big Apple Circus!"

I was tempted to say, "Were you a clown?" because I was mad at her for interrupting our private conversation. But all I said was, "Why *is* New York called the Big Apple anyway?"

None of us knew, not even Genius Justin.

Mathematically,
Mel

April 20

Dear Diary:

From Miguel:

MELANIE:

I AM IN MY FATHER'S OFFICE.

YOU ASKED WHERE I HAVE GONE ON VACATION. GALICIA. IT

41

IS A PRETTY AREA IN SPAIN WHERE THE RAIN IS SO FINE AND
GENTLE THAT IT DOES NOT SOAK THINGS, IT MAKES THEM TO
SPARKLE. THE RAIN IS CALLED MOJABOBOS, WHICH MEANS
WET FOOLS. THIS IS BECAUSE A FOOL MIGHT COMPLAIN, "I AM
WET!" BUT OTHERS LIKE THE MAGIC MIST.

MAYBE SOMEDAY YOU COME AND SEE MORE OF MY COUN-
TRY, YES?

CON CARIÑO,

MIGUEL

Yes! But I didn't know what Con cariño (Cone Care E
Nyo) meant, and I couldn't find the Spanish dictionary
anywhere. Finally I asked Mom. She said, "With care" or
"With affection." I asked her whether it seemed funny
that Miguel starts his e-mails "Melanie:" instead of "Dear
Melanie." She said, "Not in Spain."

Here's what I think,
For e-mail or ink:
A colon is formal;
A comma is normal.

Con cariño,

Melanie

April 21

Diary:

Central Park is in bloom right now. We walked across the Bow Bridge and saw herons, red-winged blackbirds, kids playing Frisbee, and dog walkers walking big Labradors, little terriers, cute spaniels, fluffy collies, crinkly pugs, stocky bulldogs, and dainty poodles, all wagging their long or stubby tails. I also saw couples rowing boats. It made me want to rush home and write to Miguel. So I did!

Dear Miguel,

We say "April showers bring May flowers," but New York has been beautiful all month! We live in an apartment, so we think of the parks as our backyard. Riverside Park is near us, and right now its trees are pink and look like strawberry ice cream cones.

The biggest park is Central Park. It has a zoo, theater, turtle pond, swimming pool, reservoir, fountains, and places to fish, ice skate, play tennis, and bird-watch. There is even an old old old obelisk called Cleopatra's Needle and a lake for riding a gondola—or rowing boats.

Remember when we did that in Madrid? I do!

Con cariño,

Melanie

44

My e-mail was already long (because I kept thinking of things to add), and I was just about to press Send when, for better or worse, my fingers typed a P.S. before my brain could stop them.

P.S. Don't take this the wrong way, but would you mind putting a comma after my name instead of a colon? In America, commas are more personal. ¡Gracias!

The second I pressed Send, I wished I hadn't. First of all, I'm not *that* big on parks, so why did I go on and on as though I were Little Miss Nature Girl? And worse, why oh why did I correct his punctuation??? Who cares if he writes "Melanie," or "Melanie:"? Now that I've corrected him, I'll be lucky if he writes me at all!

What was I thinking?

NOT THINKING,
MINDLESS MEL

an hour L8r (I am using my penlight)

I couldn't fall asleep so I called Mom to come tuck me and Hedgehog in again. I said, "Is it bad if I think about Miguel a lot?"

She smiled. "Not if you enjoy thinking about him. I guess it would be bad if thinking about him made you unhappy."

"Will you lie down with me?" I don't ask her to as much as I used to, so Mom didn't say no, she just took off her shoes and stretched out. Problem is, she fell right to sleep and I'm still wide awake.

April 24
after school

Dear Diary,

I got a detention today. It was so not fair! Cecily and I both had to miss recess, but Suze didn't. She always gets other people in trouble. And gets away with it!

Our big crime was that in assembly, we were listening to a boring speaker who wouldn't stop speaking. So at

46

the exact same time, we each crossed our left leg over our right leg, then crossed our right leg over our left leg, then rested our chin on our right hand, then rested our chin on our left hand. Then we all leaned forward and pulled our right earlobe and looked deep in thought.

The teacher noticed us and got mad. It wasn't even our real homeroom teacher—it was a sub. A sub with a bow tie and a unibrow. (If it had been Mr. Roberts, we would not have dared copy each other!)

Well, detention wasn't so so so bad because of two reasons.

1. Missing recess isn't as serious as being sent to Principal Gemunder's office—which I never have been. Not once.

2. I was inside with Cecily (which is fun), not by myself (which can get lonely), and not with Cecily and Ooze Face (which can get annoying).

But I'm still mad at Suze because the leg crossing was *her* idea, so she should have gotten in trouble too! I'm also mad because in homeroom, she and Cecily were making this secret chart grading boys on stuff like Looks and Brains and Niceness, and Suze said, "I was thinking about you and Miguel, and no offense, but isn't it easy to have a faraway boyfriend? You can just send love letters—or love e-mails—and pretend everything is perfect, since you never actually see each other."

Cecily said I shouldn't worry and that Suze is probably jealous. So why am I letting what she said get to me? Is it because it's a teeny tiny bit true? I doubt Suze is jealous, but if she is, it would be because Cecily and I have been best friends half our lives!

Anyway, I got to Spanish class early and Justin asked, "How come you weren't on turf?" Turf is what we call the fake green grass on our school's fenced-in roof.

I was surprised Justin had even noticed I missed recess. I told him what happened, and he started laughing—but in a nice way. While I was talking to him, he also started copying all my positions: crossing and uncrossing his legs, propping up his chin, and touching his earlobe.

If Matt the Brat had done that, it would have made me crazy. But since it was Justin, it made me smile.

48

P.S. I wrote a poem called "Detention Prevention."

If you don't want to miss recess,
When Suze says "Do it," don't say yes.
That's my new rule——no more, no less!

April 27

Dear Diary,

An e-mail!!!

Third Friday in a row! Does Miguel go to his dad's office only on Fridays? If so, I wish he'd say so. Magazines say a little mystery is good for romance, but when I don't know what's going on, I just worry.

A good thing about e-mail is that it's always convenient—it's not like a doorbell or a phone that can ring when you don't want to be interrupted. A bad thing about e-mail, at least for me, is that since e-mail can be so fast, it feels funny when it's not fast. By "funny," I mean the opposite!

Today, getting Miguel's e-mail made me want to half

laugh, half cry, and half smother my computer with *besitos*. (Justin a.k.a. Mr. Math would point out that that's one half too many!)

Miguel wrote:

> DEAR MELANIE,,,
> NOW THAT I KNOW THAT YOU LIKE SPRING FLOWERS, I SEND YOU A BOUQUET OF TULIPS. THE FLOWERS OF A VIRTUAL BOUQUET CAN TO CHANGE COLOR. I AM SENDING THEM TO YOU YELLOW. TELL ME IF THEY CHANGE, OKAY?
> HASTA LA PRÓXIMA,
> MIGUEL
> P.S. I AM HOPING TO TELL YOU GOOD NEWS SOON.

Isn't that Sooooooo Sweeeeeet?

At first, I didn't get it. I started looking for an attachment or enclosure or link or instructions. Then I realized that with e-mail, you can send pretend presents. If someone is upset, you can offer a virtual tissue or a cyberhug.

Confession: I like the visible commas as much as the invisible bouquet!

50

Why? Because the commas are like a secret short-hand, an inside joke that's private between Miguel and me. And I like punctuation; I especially like semi-colons.

Until today, though, I'd never thought of commas as romantic!

I still wish he'd write more. I write him way more than he writes me. I probably think about him more too.

What could the good news be?

Romantically , , ,
Melanie

April 28
Saturday Morning

Dear Diary,

Maybe Suze the Ooze is right about the "perfect" thing. Maybe it is easier to think everything's perfect when you never see the person, like when it's an Internet (or international) relationship. Or both.

When girls in our grade meet boys at camp or parties

or other schools, they always say they're "perfect." When kids in our grade go out with each other, though, things get imperfect really fast, and they dump each other in two days.

I called Cecily because I actually *wanted* her to say, "Don't worry." She did. But she also said something I didn't expect. She said Suze says I talk about Miguel too much. I was about to say, "It's none of her business!" but Cecily continued, "And I kind of agree. No offense." When Cecily said, "No offense," I wanted to hang up on her!! I didn't, though; I listened. "Melanie, you don't know if you'll ever even see him again, so you should try not to obsess. You're driving yourself a little crazy. You know?"

What I knew was, I did not like Cecily and Soozy Floozy talking about me behind my back.

What I said was, "Want to sleep over tonight?"

"I can't," Cecily said. "I have plans."

"Plans?"

"Suze's sister is having a birthday party at Benihana and Suze is allowed to bring one friend."

"Oh."

"Hey, don't worry about what I said about Miguel."

"I won't." But we both knew I would.

Are they right about Miguel? And are he and I doomed as a couple? He's over twelve and a half and I'm just eleven; he's Spanish and I'm American; we're too young to visit each other alone; and there's an ocean between us with whales and sharks and minnows and octopi in it. And squid. And algae. (Not that the contents of the ocean make a difference.)

What about my friendship with Cecily? Is it doomed? Between us there's no OCEAN, but there is an OOZER. Which may be worse!

I wish Cecily agreed with me that the Oozer is a loser!

Have I been worrying about the wrong relationship? Do I have everything backward?

Saturday night

Sitting
by the

Dear Diary, , ,

Dad has been listening to Puccini and acting grumpy. Mom says he's feeling old because of his "milestone" birthday coming up. "Milestone" birthdays usually end with 0 and 5, like when you turn 40 or 50 or 75. Mom is planning a surprise party for Dad but told me not to breathe a word—not even to Matt. (I did tell Cecily.)

The opera is called *Turandot*, and a sad fact is that Puccini died before he got to finish it. It's about a man who is madly in love with a lady named Turandot. At first she is not very nice. But eventually they kiss and she gets a little nicer. The kiss warms her up a little.

I wonder what the average age of a first kiss is. The average age to start your period is around twelve or twelve and a half. But what about kissing? Is there an average age? Does anyone study that stuff? What about bras? Is there an average first bra age??

My first kiss came last month—the forehead kiss. Age eleven. When will my first lips kiss be?

By the way, I wrote Miguel back and told him the tulips had turned pink, which I hope isn't too lovey-dovey. I started the e-mail with "Dear Miguel, , ," and I was going to add a fourth comma but decided not to. (What if his commas were typos? No, no, they were on purpose, so I'm *not* going to worry about that! No one accidentally writes things three times!)

Yours, Yours, Yours,
Mel Mel Mel

P.S. I wish Cecily were here.

Sunday Evening

Dear Diary,

Cecily called this morning and said, "I'm free today. Are you?"

I said, "Yes," but I thought, **"YESSS!!!"**

Mom was going to an all-day art conference, so Matt begged Dad to take us to the Bronx Zoo, and amazing but true, he said okay. Dad likes the zoo. He said the first time he went was in 1899, when it was founded. Matt asked, "Really?" and Dad said, "No!" and Matt started hopping around singing the Raffi song about going to the zoo-zoo-zoo-how-about-you-you-you? It was tempting to smack him, but I was too happy.

On the way to the zoo, we wanted to listen to Z100 on the radio, but Dad wanted to listen to opera and he won. So Cecily, Matt, and I sat in back and took turns mouthing opera songs and making big dramatic arm gestures. We were laughing, but I was worried that Cecily might like being with Suze's big sister, who is probably mature, more than with my little brother, who is definitely NOT.

In the Congo Gorilla Forest, we watched baby gorillas copying their parents—even though their parents were doing gross things like scratching their privates, banging their chests, picking their noses, and eating with their mouths open.

After that, we went to see snakes, and Matt pressed his face to the window and stuck his tongue out to see if they'd stick their tongues out back. Some did, but it was coincidence.

Get this: He told Dad to try and Dad did! (Dad can be pretty immature for a grown-up.)

I whispered to Cecily that in monkey families, children learn bad habits from the parents, but in my family, the dad learns bad habits from the kid. She laughed. Which made me feel good. I like her laugh.

Here's what we didn't talk about: Suze. Or Miguel.

Anyway, we also saw lions and tigers and bears (oh my!) and then we dropped Cecily off at her apartment.

Now I am on our sofa and Matt is standing next to me, watching me write. He has a white mouse in his pocket—he showed me. He says mice are natural hiders; that's how they keep safe from birds of prey.

I said, "Cool."

"Did you write about the dried-up gorilla poop?"

"No way."

"Why not? That was awesome!"

"Keep your own diary, Matt!"

He mentioned gorilla poop because at the zoo, we saw a movie about a woman who studies gorillas. She came upon a clump of dried-up gorilla poop and broke it with a stick so she could learn what the gorillas had been eating.

Yeah! Right! Like I'm going to write about *that* in my diary!

Stupid Matt, now I realize I just did!!!

"I hope you're happy, Little Science Boy," I announced. "I just wrote about gorilla poop."

"Lemme see!"

I let him read what I just just just wrote.

"You called me Little Science Boy?"

"It's my diary. I can call you anything I want."

"Put in that you're an E.B.S."

"1. I am not an Evil Big Sister. 2. Why would I?"

Matt shrugged, and the little mouse peeked out of his pocket, wiggled its whiskers, blinked its teeny red eyes, and rubbed its nose with its front paws. It was so cute that we both laughed. Matt said, "Put in that I have MouseMouse in my pocket." So I just did.

Squeak squeak squeak,
Melanie, Matt, and MouseMouse

P.S.

We often go to the zoo;
We visit museums too.
Is this what tourists do?
Enjoy New York as if it's . . . NEW?

May 12

Dear Diary,

Sorry I haven't written in almost *two weeks*. First I lost you, which was terrible. (You were under the bed—as you must know!)

Then I felt too awful to write. Four things are bothering me, so I'll write them in order of badness, less bad to most bad.

1. Outside, it's done nothing but rain. Not a fine magic mist that makes things sparkle. No. A nonstop soggy downpour.

Here is a rain rectangle:

Rain Rain Rain Rain Rain
Rain Rain Rain Rain Rain
Rain Rain Rain Rain Rain
Rain Rain Rain Rain Rain
Rain Rain Rain Rain Rain

2. Inside it stinks too. Literally.

Our mice are not adorable anymore. They smell and they're gross. They're constantly trying to make babies with each other, even though they are all related! The original mom, Milkshake, is pregnant again. Her little belly keeps getting big and bumpy.

Matt has a new joke. Question: How do you make babies? Answer: Drop the y and add ies!

He showed me a book that says mice are "prolific breeders" and start breeding when they are just six weeks old. Female mice can have a litter every single month. Females who live with males are almost always pregnant. And a healthy female in captivity (meaning in a cage with no cats, owls, or hawks) can have around a hundred babies in a year. 100!!!

This could be a problem!!!

Mom and Dad made us give four of the not-so-little-anymore baby mice back to the pet store. The owner said he'd try to sell them, but I'm worried he'll sell them as snake food.

3. Cecily and Suze got their ears pierced. Together! On May 5. Cecily knows my mom won't let me until I'm twelve, but she could have asked, or waited, or at least invited me along!!

They showed me the photos of their Bonding Moment, and I told them they looked great. Which was *not* easy.

I'm starting to feel like a Big Baby around them.

Suze lives to get attention. Depending on what lunch is at school, she's either a vegetarian or not, or allergic or not. And it works—she *gets* attention. Especially from boys. Even nice ones like Justin. Maybe it's because she has long long long hair. Or because she's pretty developed for our age. Or because she has a big big big mouth. And cool clothes. Now she has earrings too. She'll probably have a dozen pairs in no time.

I think she likes Justin. Not that I care.

I know she likes Cecily. And I do care!

Last week they wore matching skirts and were laughing so loudly in the library that they got a detention. Believe it or not, I wished I'd gotten a detention too, even though that's a stupid thing to wish for.

Confession: When Suze asks, "How's your boyfriend?" I don't even know if she's being nice or making fun of me.

4. Two Fridays; zero e-mail! Need I say more?

I wrote two poems:

What do boys think about?
They are hard to figure out!

and

Violets are blue, roses are red.
Are my tulips already dead?

I realize that even virtual bouquets don't last forever. But I didn't expect mine to just plain *disappear*.

I wrote Miguel a few times about rain and school and mice. Did the e-mails even get there? If not, wouldn't they have boomeranged back? Did I write them in disappearing ink???

Invisibly,
Melaria.

May 13, SUNday but it
should be called RAINday

Dear Diary,

Suze phoned looking for Cecily. I said, "She isn't

here." She said, "What are you doing today?" I said, "Errands with my mom," then felt like a little kid for admitting that.

Later Cecily called and said, "Suze helped me go through my closet, and I have some hand-me-downs for you. My mom is about to leave them with your doorman, okay?" I said sure because I love when Cecily gives me hand-me-downs. They're usually jeans and tops and bathing suits that are too tight for her but fit me fine.

An hour later, our doorman Gustavo buzzed and said a bag had been dropped off, so I went down and said *gracias* and brought the bag up to my room.

Well, life is full of surprises because inside the bag marked Melanie Martin (which had a sweater in it) was a second bag, and inside it was . . . a bunch of bras! Outgrown bras! I can't believe Cecily has already outgrown her first bras! And I can't believe she let Suze go through her clothes and help fill up a bra bag for me.

Talk about humiliating!

"Want to go shopping?" Mom asked, popping her head into my room, even though she hadn't knocked and I keep asking her to.

I shoved the bras in the back of my sock drawer, slammed the drawer shut, and said, "Sure."

Out we went. We bought invitations for Dad's party, then Mom offered to buy me a top at Morris Bros. I wished she'd offered to buy me a bra, but why would she have?

At the store, Mom picked out five tops that I would *never* wear in a million years. I said, "I can pick out my own stuff," and Mom backed off.

I chose two tops, but Mom said one looked "trampy" and the other was "too revealing."

Finally we found one we both liked and Mom bought it. It's silky blue. And I'm happy about that.

But how can I be truly happy when things are weird with my so-called best friend and my so-called boyfriend?

Here's how I really feel: like a dried-up Christmas tree.

You know how on sidewalks in early January, there are evergreens everywhere? Tired-out trees lying on their sides waiting to be taken away by garbage trucks? Weeks earlier, those same trees had presents under them, and stars on top of them, and they gleamed with lights, ornaments, tinsel, and candy canes. Each one smelled fresh and piney and made someone somewhere feel joyful and lighthearted.

Then, boom, just like that, it was: Time's up, party's over.

Happens every year, but it always comes as a sad surprise.

Well, *that's* how I feel. Like a forgotten Christmas tree.

They say nothing lasts forever. But I wish holidays did. And first love! And best friendship!!

I wish things had stayed the same,
although I know that wish is lame.

In English last week, we learned the word "chagrin," which is when you feel sad or disappointed. Well, "chagrin" has "grin" buried in it. And now, if I try, I bet I can find something positive buried deep inside all this.

Got it: Deep down, even when used-up evergreens are everywhere, you know, you still know, that Christmas will come again. Because Christmas always does. Year after year.

And deep down, even when it is rainy, you know the

sun is up there somewhere shining away. Because that's what it does, day after day.

Miserably yours anyway,
Melanie in Minor Chords

P.S. I wrote an unjolly poem shaped like a Christmas tree.

I
know
I should
cheer up. What
I do not know is
how!

bedtime

Dear Diary,

Dad took Matt to a little-kid movie, so Mom and I quickly worked on the invitations to his surprise party. (Shhhh!) Mom says doing something creative is "spirit lifting," and I confess, it *was* fun to doodle party hats and birthday cakes on all the envelopes.

Writing in you helped too.

Doodlingly,
M

May 14
before school

Dear Diary,

I don't know why Miguel isn't writing, but I've made a decision. I'm not going to keep writing him. Here's my new rule for myself: I will not write Miguel. I will not write Miguel!

> YOURS WITH DETERMINATION,
>   MEL

5/14 P.M.

DD,

iwnwm
iwnwm
iwnwm
iwnwm

xo
mm

Dear Diary,

I went online to see if Miguel had written (I'm weak, I admit!), and Cecily had forwarded me a cool e-mail. Usually I get the stupid kind that ends by saying if you forward them to ten friends, you'll have good luck, but if you don't, you'll wake up dead. (You know what I mean.)

I hate those e-mails because I don't want to wake up dead, but if I keep forwarding them to friends, soon I won't have *any* friends.

Her e-mail said:

> If the frist and lsat lettres of a wrod are in the rihgt plcae, the odrer of the ohter ltteres deosn't mttaer. Why? Bceuase poelpe dno't raed leettr by ltteer. Tehy raed wrod by wrod.

I was just figuring it out when Justin IMed me. He wrote **sup**. I wrote n2m (for not too much). He wrote **r u ok?** I was surprised and wrote yes y? He wrote **u seemed quiet 2day.**

Well, I didn't want to blame the rain, Miguel, or the bag of bras, so I decided to try to be funny, even though trying to be funny doesn't always work.

I wrote: a math word problem is bothering me.

He wrote: **r u kidding?**

I wrote: In March, Melanie Martin had a pair of mice. In April, they became ten mice. Four were given away, but the others kept getting pregnant. How soon will Melanie Martin have one million mice?

Justin wrote: **lol**

Which actually made me smile—
for the first time in a while

I liked picturing him laughing out loud, so I wrote i am about 2 send u something Cecily sent me.

He wrote **k** and I cut and pasted the thing about lagnugae. He wrote **incerdilbe!**

I sent a smiley.

He wrote: **i looked up big apple**

I typed: u did?

Then he wrote about different ways New York might have gotten nicknamed the Big Apple. It might have to do with the apple that tempted Adam and Eve (even though the Bible never said the fruit was definitely an apple). Or with horse races because winning horses were given big apples. Or with a jazz club and dance club in Harlem called the Big Apple. Whatever the reason, in 1971 the nickname was used for New York tourism and it stuck.

I wrote: I nveer kenw taht!

He sent a smiley.

I wanted to keep writing, but Dad yelled, "Dinnertime!" so I wrote dinenritme g2g and he wrote **wut's deessrt?** and I wrote mybae aplpe pi! and we signed off.

Signing OFF,
Malenie in the Big 🍎

P.S. Miguel and I had commas as our inside e-mail joke; do Justin and I have fnuny spelinlg?

P.P.S. New poem:

My little mice are not shy——
All they do is multiply!

Dear Diary,

Suze is ruining my life—which has not been 100 percent perfect lately anyway!

Today on the lunch line, she whispered, "I asked Justin if he likes you."

"What?! Why???" I swear, I almost dropped my lunch tray, Salisbury steak, mashed potatoes, carrots, and all.

"Because sometimes it seems like he does."

"We're just friends!!" She raised one eyebrow (which she loves to do since no one else in our class can) and smiled an I-know-more-than-you-do smile, so I asked, "What did he say?"

"He said he might like you a little, or he might like you someday, but right now, he likes a girl from camp."

I wanted to die. "Suze, I wish you hadn't asked him!"

"I was curious. You're not the only one who thinks he's cute."

"Who said I think he's cute?"

"Oh, c'mon, Melanie, he *is* cute. That's not even up for debate!"

"You didn't tell him I asked you to ask him, did you?"

"No! I wouldn't pretend to be your messenger. I asked because *I* wanted to know."

She sat down, so I did too, but part of me wanted to mash my already-mashed potatoes into her face.

"Since he mentioned the camp girl," she continued, "I told him about your long-distance boyfriend."

"You didn't!" I wish she'd never moved here!!

"I did. I couldn't tell if he was surprised or disappointed or if he didn't care one way or the other. As my dad would say, he has a poker face."

"I can't believe you! And Suze, I don't even know if I have a boyfriend. Miguel hasn't e-mailed in over two weeks." Why I was telling this to the class blabbermouth, I have no idea.

"Two weeks?" She took a sip from her milk carton and jiggled her Jell-O. "No offense, but that is pretty long. Think he broke up with you and forgot to tell you?"

"What do you mean?"

"I read that some boys do that. Of course, if he did, then at least you wouldn't be 'taken,' so you could ask Justin out if you wanted to."

"But I *don't* want to!"

"Oh, good. That's what I wanted to find out, because *I* might ask him out, which I wouldn't if you and he already liked each other. I mean, I wouldn't want you to be mad at me." She looked up and the gold stud in her ear gleamed.

I couldn't bring myself to tell her that I was already mad at her! Really mad! Furious mad! Boiling mad!

I took a bite of potato, but I couldn't eat. So I just sat there, trying not to cry and trying to get the potato bite to go down past the lump in my throat. Across the cafeteria, I saw Justin walking toward the exit. Normally I might have looked up and waved and smiled and said hi. But all I could do was stare down and hope he didn't see me see him. Which I don't think he did. He was looking straight ahead. Maybe he was trying to avoid eye contact too??

Has Suze messed things up with both Cecily *and* Justin?

My eyes started burning, and tears blurred up my carrots and potatoes. Somehow I blinked them back. The last thing you want to do in a school cafeteria is cry!!

I took a sip of milk, mumbled, "I'm outta here," got up, and left.

Suze called out, "What's the matter? Is something wrong? Hey, what about your tray?"

I didn't answer, just rushed through the lunchroom. I could feel everyone looking but I made it through the crowded doorway and into the hall—where I practically bumped into . . . Cecily!

"What's the matter? Is something wrong?" she asked. They were the exact same questions Suze had just asked, but from Cecily they sounded nice, not horrible. I motioned for Cecily to go with me to the girls' room. A third grader was inside, but she took one look at me and left in a hurry.

"Cecily," I said, "Suze asked Justin if he liked me!"

"Omigod! You're kidding!" She looked shocked—which was better than her trying to defend Suze. "What'd he say?" I told her, and she didn't even say, "Don't worry." Which worried me.

I told her the rest of our conversation too. She listened and said that last week, Suze had asked her to ask Justin who he liked, but she'd said she didn't want to.

Cecily also said, "You have a little potato on your lip." I looked in the mirror (I looked awful!!) and wiped the potato away. The least the Oozer could have done was tell me I was wearing lunch!

It is now 8:30 P.M., but I have finished my homework and checked my e-mail and there's nothing on TV so I'm going to bed pathetically early.

Matt has been singing and jumping around, and I told him to keep quiet. He said he'd try, but that he's bad at keeping quiet.

I said, "So is Suze."

He said, "What?"

I said, "Never mind."

> If you ever have news,
> do not blab it to Suze.
> There is too much to lose.

Sweet dreams (or at least No nightmares),
   Melanie (and Hedgie)

P.S. I just took off my silver fan necklace that Miguel gave me. I've worn it for over six weeks straight, which is way longer than I usually wear jewelry.

P.P.S. iwnwm

It stinks to have a guy I miss.
I'd rather have another kiss
and keep on wearing his necklace.

same night, elevenish

Maybe I'm a drama queen,
but I think Suze is mean, mean, mean!

May 17
after school

Dear Diary,

Justin and I are talking a little, but I feel awkward around him, and I think he feels the same way. In math, I asked him to explain something and he did, but without looking at me. If I didn't already know his eyes are greenish hazel, I'd have no idea what color they are.

In Spanish, he asked me to help him pronounce

some words. Like, toes are "fingers of the foot" or *dedos del pie* (Day Dose Del Pyay). And neck is *cuello* (Quay Yo). And lips are *labios* (La B Yose), which for some reason felt embarrassing.

More than help with math and Spanish, I think Justin and I both want things to go back to normal. But what is normal between us? Maybe we have to find a new normal.

Unnormally,
mm

@round midnight ☾
with my penlight

Dear Diary,

Owwwww! I fell out of bed. On my head! I'm way too old to do that but I did that.

Mom didn't have a normal ice pack, so she handed me a bag of frozen peas, which I wore like a cold bumpy hat. Then she sat down to keep me company.

"I'm sorry if I woke you," I said, reaching for my glasses.

"No need to apologize." Mom kissed me. "I was read-ing. In fact, I just learned something. Nowadays, when artists depict someone with glasses, they may be saying that the person is smart. But in the Middle Ages, when a subject was wearing glasses, the artist was saying that the person was *foolish*—that he couldn't even see with his own eyes!"

I sat there with glasses on my nose and peas on my head, and I think Mom realized (a little late) that I was feeling foolish enough without her new factoid. To tell you the truth, I was about to tell *her* the truth about how everything is going wrong. But just when I was about to speak up, she stood up.

Mom took the pea bag off my head
and tucked me back into my bed.

So here I am, alone again. And here's what I think: I might give up on Miguel. But not on Cecily.

Your hurt friend,

Mel-A-Moron

P.S.

I admit I feel some sorrow,
But there's hope about tomorrow.

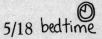

5/18 bedtime

Dear Diary,

   Cecily e-mailed me, so I e-mailed Justin:

    Count the F's:

    "Friendship comes from the pleasure

    of knowing someone well, a mutual

    sense of fun, and, if possible, the

    sharing of common interests."

    Ffffffondly,

    M.

   P.S. Justin is good at math, but will he find all the F's? I didn't. Even if he answers wrong, it could still help our friendship.

5/19 at 5:19

home

Dear Diary,

I had an orthodontist appointment and forgot to remember my retainer. Which annoyed Mom. But walking
up Fifth Avenue, I said, "Want to stop at the Met?"
Which thrilled her.

To Mom, the Met is like a big enormous treasure chest.
Or a wonderful time machine. Even Matt likes the an-
cient mummies, knights in shining armor, graffiti on the
Temple of Dendur, and chipped statues with missing
hands, heads, and you-know-whats. Until today, though,
I don't think I'd ever been the one to suggest a visit.

In front of the Met, Mom handed me a five-dollar bill
and I bought us two big, soft, warm, salty pretzels. Mom
said, "Check the change," then asked, "Anything you
want to see?"

"Maybe that Goya boy?" I'd been thinking about that
Goya lady from Mom's field trip. The devoted duchess
with the "Only Goya" ring.

Did she ever take her ring off? I took my necklace off.

"Don Manuel Osorio Manrique de Zuñiga," Mom said,

because she actually knows these things. We went up all the outside stairs and all the inside stairs until we were standing in front of him.

It's weird. Every time I look at Don Manuel, *he* stays the same. But *I* notice something completely new.

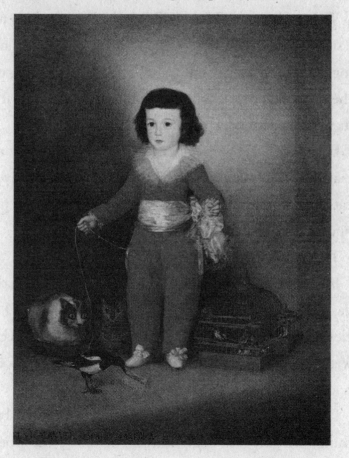

When I was little, I liked that he was my age and all dressed up with a white bow and a pet bird on a leash. After that, I saw the cage of other birds—six little finches. Later I noticed that in the pet bird's beak is a calling card: a paper rectangle with a palette and Goya's curly signature.

Well, today was STRANGE. Maybe I was looking for a sign or something, but it's like I finally "got" the painting, and it is *not* what I thought! The light is shining on the boy's sweet face, and you think you're looking at a lucky kid with a cool pet magpie.

But nooooo. That is only the beginning! Besides one magpie and six finches, there are three big yellow-eyed cats that are NOT in a cage. They are staring at the pet bird, and soon there may not be a pet bird!

This boy is in for a surprise!

Is it because of Blanquito in the dishwasher that I have dead birds on the brain? Or is it because now that I'm eleven, I'm old enough to see Goya's "dark side"? (He went from painting happy-happy scenes to creepy spooky nudie ones of ghosts and cannibals and wars.)

Dad says kids see the world in black and white, but things are gray and complicated. Mom says the world isn't gray; it's colorful. All I can say is that the painting is a beautiful BEFORE, but the AFTER could be ugly. Pretty soon, that little boy could be sobbing his eyes out!

This week in English, we learned about foreshadowing. That's when an author writes, "The swimmers did not hear the distant thunder" or "No one guessed that the car's brakes were faulty," or when any sentence makes you go "Uh-oh."

Well, that whole painting made me go "Uh-oh"!

It was as if Goya was daring us to see that in real life, happy endings are not guaranteed. And maybe telling us to appreciate the present?

Mom said I'd made "a perceptive interpretation."

Before we left, I took a final look at poor Don Manuel of the long last name and the maybe-about-to-be-dead pet bird. Too bad he couldn't just grab his bird and run. But the paint was dry. He was totally stuck.

Not me, though. I am *not* stuck. I might have wanted to fall in love, but I never wanted to fall into a rut.

Well, if I got myself into it, I can get myself out!

On the way home, Mom the Mind Reader asked if I'd heard from Miguel. I said, "Not for three weeks."

"That's not so long, Kitty Cat."

"Yes it is. It's eternity."

She said that in the olden days before e-mail, pen pals traded letters just a few times a year, and no one expected constant instant answers.

"But now they do," I said. "It's different."

"Maybe. Or maybe Spanish time is different from American time. Or boy time is different from girl time."

"Doesn't matter anyway," I said. "I'm swearing off boys. Life is stressful enough."

Mom smiled. "You remind me of someone."

"Who?"

"Whom."

I rolled my eyes. "WHOM?"

"Atlas."

"Huh?"

"You know, on Fifth Avenue, across from Saint Patrick's Cathedral. The statue of the man holding up the whole wide world."

"I look like Atlas?"

"You're cuter! But you both carry a lot of weight on your shoulders." Mom didn't mean it meanly, but it felt like when spell check suggests Meanie for Melanie—and never even adds "No offense." (Of course, if it *did* add "No offense," I'd be extra offended because I'd think it was picking up cues from Ooze!) Mom continued, "Cupcake, Atlas can't put down his load, but maybe you can." She put her hand on my neck and gave me a mini backrub.

You know what? It felt pretty good.

YOURS with room for improvement,
    Museum Mel

Dear Diary,

I've been working on a poem with imagery (which we studied in Writing Workshop):

> The young boy in the perfect pose
> is wearing fancy blood-red clothes
> and has white and lacy bows
> on his collar, belt, and toes.
> He's unaware that danger shows.
> But thorns do grow on every rose,
> and even children have their woes,
> and birds know cats aren't friends—they're foes.

Yours in poetry and prose
(and in highs as well as lows),
Mel who has a two—inch nose

May 21

Dear Diary,

Justin ignored me in school today.

Yours,

Melanie the Ignorable

May 22

Dear Diary,

Cecily said I should just talk to Justin, so in Spanish I wrote a note that said, "Did you get my e-mail?" He wrote: "I haven't been online." So I whispered, "Too bad—you missed a friendly e-mail from me." I even made myself smile. He seemed curious, so I scribbled out the whole "Friendship" thing and told him to count the F's. He wrote right back: "3." I said, "Double plus one!" He said, "7??" I nodded and he looked again carefully and found the other F's. He wrote: "Amzanig."

Señora Barrios got mad.

But it was worth it.

Fickly yours?

Melanie of the Upper West Side of the city of New York (3 F's!)

Dear Diary,

Remember I told you about the boy who didn't know something bad was about to happen? Well, I'm the girl who didn't know something *good* was about to happen!

The phone rang and I picked it up.

"May Lah Nee?"

"Miguel???"

"Hello, May Lah Nee!" He sounded nervous. "I have never telephoned overseas. But our computer was not functioning and—"

"Really?? I'm so glad!" That came out wrong because I didn't mean I was glad his computer was broken. "Is it fixed?" I asked.

"Yes." Miguel laughed. "However, I call you because I have my good news."

"What is it?"

"My Uncle Angel has a trip for business to New York after my school year, and my father said that if it is okay with your family, I could visit you for one week if you are not too busy. Would this be possible?"

Possible? It would be *perfecto*! I said so and then we put our parents on the phone.

All I can say now is: Uncle Angel is an angel! I can't believe it!! One minute I was feeling like an idiot for caring about a faraway guy, and the next I'm about to be a Big Apple tour guide! Mom talked to Dad, and now everyone agrees that Miguel's visit or *visita* (B C Ta) sounds fun.

I wrote:

```
Dear Miguel,,,
    I can't believe you're coming to New
York City! That is fantástico! I want
to show you the Empire State Building
and also places that regular tourists
do not know about. I am going to start
planning! I will write you again very
soon!!!
    ¡Hasta pronto!
    Melanie
```

I tried to send the e-mail, but for some reason, my computer said the system wasn't "responding" and it couldn't connect to the Internet. It was soooo frustrating! I tried to send it two more times, then gave up and pressed Send Later. After dinner, I clicked on Mail Waiting to Be Sent and sent my message across the squiddy, shark-filled, algae-dotted ocean.

But guess what? I just checked my Sent Mail, and my e-mail to Miguel was there. *Four* times!!!! It *did* get sent all those times after all! Which means it is now in Miguel's New Mail box *four* times!

Last time Miguel got four e-mails from me, at least they were different. This time, they are identical. I'd said, "I will write you very soon," and then I wrote him very very very very soon over and over and over and over.

AArrgghh!
Mortified,
Melanie x Four

5/24
bedtime

Dear Diary,
Miguel wrote:

90

MELANIE,

MELANIE,

MELANIE,

MELANIE,

THANK YOU THANK YOU THANK YOU THANK YOU

FOR YOUR

MESSAGE MESSAGE MESSAGE MESSAGE.

MIGUEL

MIGUEL

MIGUEL

MIGUEL

That made me feel better better better better.

At dinner, Mom said that while Miguel's uncle will be working in New York, Miguel's parents will be working on their marriage by taking a trip alone, just them. She also mentioned that on the fourth night of Miguel's visit, she and Dad already have concert tickets, but that the rest of the time, we can all show Miguel around together. Dad may even take one or two vacation days.

I wanted to say, "I can show him around myself,"

but I'm not exactly an independent teenager or anything. Not yet anyway!

During dinner, I got out a lined piece of paper and said we should plan out Miguel's trip. It was exciting to think of all the possibilities! Everyone started talking fast and making suggestions.

Matt said, "How about a Yankees game? Or Madison Square Garden?"

Mom said, "How about the Met? And the Roof Garden?"

Matt said, "We could go rock climbing at Chelsea Piers!"

I said, "Or have lunch at Chelsea Market!"

Dad said, "Let's start with something one hundred percent New York: the Entire State Building." Matt used to call it that when he was littler.

We all approved the idea and I said, "Miguel would have liked that boat party."

"He'd like the *Intrepid*," Matt said. "Or South Street Seaport!"

"Let's take him to a Broadway show," I suggested.

"We could also just walk around different neighborhoods," Mom said. "Soho. Greenwich Village. Gramercy Park. Battery Park."

"What about *Central* Park?" Matt's eyes lit up. "We could climb Balto and go to Belvedere Castle and see the Marionette Theater and ride the merry-go-round."

"Miguel is a little old for merry-go-rounds," I pointed out, even though I *could* almost picture the two of us going side by side and round and round on the carousel's fancy, hand-carved horses. Truth is, I suddenly wanted to show Miguel E̲v̲e̲r̲y̲t̲h̲i̲n̲g̲. I was thinking of Bloomie's for shopping and American Girl Place for tea and Serendipity 3 for frozen hot chocolate—but then I realized they're better for girls and I was out of my mind.

Was I thinking, "What would Miguel like best?" or just imagining a fantasy guest?

Mostly I was thinking how nice it would be to have some time alone—the two of us. Without my family. (Very nice!)

"Wait! I've got it!" Matt said, as though he'd just hatched the idea of a lifetime. "The Macy's Parade! Miguel could see Santa!!"

"The parade is on Thanksgiving, you turkey," I said. Matt gobbled, but you could tell even he was embarrassed to have said something so extraordinarily *estúpido* (S 2 Pee Dough).

Dad said, "We'll pack in as much as we can. But he won't see everything. And we don't have to plan every minute. It's okay to wing it."

"We can go with the flow," Mom agreed. She added that the trip would be good for Miguel's English because he'd learn expressions like "wing it" and "go with the flow."

Me, I like to *plan* things, not wing things. And I like to *know*, not flow. Still it's true that:

Here in NYC,
there is a lot to see!
If you have just a week,
You will get just a peek!

Excitedly,
Manhattan
Mel

94

P.S. Mom and Dad's passports arrived in today's mail. The passports are navy blue with silver eagles, and the photos now have blue stripes on them and red stars next to them.

I'm afraid Dad's photo is even worse than I remembered. Mom was right. Dad should have opened his eyes a teeny bit more because he does look a teeny bit old.

Just being honest.

May 25
before school

Dear Diary,

I wrote Miguel:

```
Hi Miguel,
How are you?
How was your day?
Are you ready for the trip?
Are you getting packed and excited?
Did you like the shape of this e-mail?
XO,
mm
```

Dear Diary,

  Miguel wrote back:

> ¡HOLA MELANIE!
>
> YOU MAKE ME SMILE.
>
> I LIKE TRIÁNGULOS TOO.
>
> I'M NOT READY FOR MY TRIP,
>
> BUT I AM GETTING CURIOUS. TELL ME:
>
> WHAT IS THE FIRST THING YOU WILL SHOW ME?

I felt like answering, "My smile!" But of course I didn't!!

Melonline.

P.S.

I like a guy
and he likes me.
what's my name?
It's May Lah Nee!

:-)

Dear Diary,

It was a pretty day and Mom offered to buy me a Popsicle if I took an afternoon walk with her.

"That's a bribe," I said.

"It is," she agreed, and out we went.

We walked along the Boat Basin west of Riverside Park and watched the boats bobbing on the Hudson River. A few floating ducks and flying seagulls were enjoying the sunshine too, and my pink Popsicle got very drippy.

Mom said, "Cecily hasn't been over much lately. Everything okay?"

I shrugged. "Not really." I told her all about Soozer the Loser. I even said that Suze was supposed to wait before replacing her starter studs with new earrings, but that she'd made the switch this morning, then spent the whole school day making sure *everyone* noticed. I didn't add, "Especially the boys."

At first Mom just listened. Then she said, "You know what, Sweet Pea? I asked about *Cecily*, and the

97

only person you're telling me about is Suze. You have to focus on your friends, not your enemies."

Maybe she had a point, but I said, "Sometimes you just don't get it."

Mom sighed and led us to a sculpture of Eleanor Roosevelt. "You know who she is, right?" I shrugged because I wasn't sure if I did or if I didn't. "She was F.D.R.'s wife and a famous first lady, and also quite a writer. She said one of my favorite quotes."

"Which one?"

"No one can make you feel inferior without your consent."

"Huh?"

"It means *you* are in charge of *your* feelings. You can't give other people the power to make you feel bad about yourself. If Suze isn't nice, let that be her problem, not your problem."

"Easier said than done."

Mom put her arm around me. "I can't disagree," she said, which is a double negative.

POSITIVELY YOURS,
M.M.

Dear Diary,

I must be growing. When I woke up, my feet looked so far away that my first thought was:

Whose toes
are those?!

Off to school—

M

:⸳ ⸳ ⸳ ☽ ⸳:
bedtime on
the very last day
of the month of May

Dear Diary,

I have way too many butterflies in my stomach! If I flapped my arms, I'd wind up at the top of the Empire State Building!

Here's what I can't figure out:

If one person is thinking about another person,

does the other person think about that person back? If one person feels a spark, does the other person too? Is it the same spark or a bigger or smaller spark? And how can you be sure?

I like to be sure!

Maybe it depends. Do questions like these even have answers? Are they math problems? Or chemistry problems?

The reason I'm asking is because I went online and Justin IMed me. I felt kind of warm just seeing his name.

He wrote: **hi**

So I wrote: `hi`

He wrote: **r u going 2 spring fling?**

I had to read that over about ten times because I couldn't believe he was asking. Spring Fling is the end-of-the-year fifth-grade dance in our gym, and it's supposed to be really fun.

I felt bad for not sending an instant reply, but I didn't know what to answer.

First of all, was he asking IF I was going or was he asking me TO go? I considered calling Cecily for advice, but I couldn't leave Justin hanging there.

Finally I wrote: r u? which I thought was pretty safe.

Now *he* took forever to reply (well, sixty seconds at least). Then he wrote: **c u there!**

So I wrote: great! With one matching exclamation point. I was going to add another, but I figured one was good.

I saved the conversation and signed off, and now it's a Butterfly Zone in my stomach. Some are American butterflies and some are Spanish *mariposas* (Mar E Poe Sahss).

Spring Fling is coming up in nine days.

Then school ends.

Then Miguel comes.

Counting down,

Melanieeeeeeee

Dear Diary,

Did Justin ask other people if they were going too? Was he taking a poll of the whole grade so he could help the committee figure out how much pizza to order? Or did he just ask me?

I called Cecily.

"Did Justin ask if you're going to the dance?"

"No. Why?"

"No reason . . ."

"Wait! Omigod! Did he ask you?!"

"I'm not sure."

"You're not sure?"

I started to explain, then said, "Go online and I'll show you." I pasted in our conversation and sent it to her even though I know that's against "e-mail etiquette."

"What do you think?" I asked.

"I think you should wear that silky blue top you showed me!" She laughed and added that she was wearing a new shirt to the dance and was going to change her earrings that day for the first time ever.

I was tempted to ask, "What's Suze wearing?" but I didn't want to ooze up our phone call. By the way, one of Suze's earlobes got a little infected and is a teeny bit pink and crusty. Hee hee. (That's mean. I know.)

Yours,
    Meanie Melanie

June 5 in bed

DD,

Quiet Question:
    Is it unwise
    to like two guys?

Love,
    Mel

June 8 after dinner

Dear Diary,

Tomorrow is the big dance. I keep wishing I had the guts to go up to Justin and say, "Are we friends—or more?" But 1. I don't, and 2. I wouldn't want him to ask *me* that, especially since Miguel is coming in

103

exactly ten days and I don't know if he and I are friends—or more.

I don't even know if Cecily and I are best friends—or less.

Today was Field Day. After lunch, Cecily and I were talking about how instant messages can sometimes be confusing. She said, "Suze and I once got in a dumb fight because we were going to a movie and I typed: 'I can't wait!' and Suze took it wrong."

"What do you mean?"

"She thought I was saying, 'Sorry, but I cannot wait,' when all I meant was, 'I'm looking forward to it! Can't wait!!' She got all mad for nothing. And another time," Cecily continued (I have to say, I was enjoying this conversation), "I wrote: 'I resent it,' and she thought I resented something when, really, I meant I'd sent a message two times not just one time. And once" (Cecily was on quite a roll), "I wrote: 'So there,' meaning, 'I am soooo there,' but she thought I meant it like, 'Ha ha so there.'"

I felt like saying, "I told you Suze is trouble," but I didn't.

I felt like saying, "So never IM her," but I didn't.

I felt like saying, "You said I talk about Miguel a lot but you talk about Suze a lot," but I didn't say that either.

I mostly just listened, then said, "I guess things are clearer when you're actually with someone, person to person."

Yesterday, I took a magazine quiz called, "Are You a Worrier?" It said some people worry too much and some don't worry enough. I scored my answers, and you can guess where I landed!

Well, I wish I *weren't* a worrier. I even worry about worrying! But I am trying to change, to worry about certain things instead of *everything*. I am also trying to take Mom's advice about trying to care about my friendship with Cecily instead of Cecily's friendship with Suze, or my enemyship with Suze.

Your Almost Sixth Grader Friend,
Mellie the Mature (today anyway)

P.S. Here's a poem I've been working on:

Some people drive you crazy.
Some people keep you sane.
Which ones should you worry about?
The answer should be plain.

late late late June 9

Dear Diary,

The dance was almost over. Justin had danced a lot (including twice with Suze, who asked him), and I'd danced only once (with Norb, who asked me).

I was about to ask Cecily if I should ask Justin to dance, but then Suze the Ooze came to schmooze and I didn't want to ask Justin in front of her. She said, "Come with me to the girls' room." She was including me, I guess, but Cecily went and I didn't want to.

So I just stood there, all alone, trying to find the courage to approach Justin.

The dj announced that the next song would be the last dance and said it would be "a slow one." I looked up, and suddenly Justin was coming straight toward me! Our eyes met and our eyes smiled then our mouths smiled and he got all the way up to me and I felt tingly and it was as if we were moving in slow motion and the music started and he took my hand and pulled me gently onto the dance floor and rested his other hand on my back and I could feel his fingers on the back of my silky top and I didn't know where to put my hands but I put them behind his shoulders and I leaned my head toward his and my ear touched his ear and I closed my eyes and I could feel his warm breath and we kind of swayed silently until the song was over and all the lights went on.

If I didn't have a bf in Spain and he didn't have a gf in camp, I'd probably let myself think about tonight forever.

Sigh sigh sigh.

Live from
New York,
  it's Saturday night—

    Melanie

                                                    June 12
                                                  bedtime

Dear Diary,

School is over!!!

We cleaned out our lockers and said tons of goodbyes (Justin gave me a fast hug) and got our grades. I did really well in English and Spanish and pretty well in everything else.

Now we have the whole summer to sleep late and stay up late and read whatever books we want.

After dinner, we four M's walked down Broadway to get ice cream cones. On the walk back, Mom asked for a bite of my cone. I said, "You should have gotten your own."

Mom said, "C'mon, Mel. I gave birth to you!"

Dad said, "It's true. For nine months, your mother drank an awful lot of milk."

Matt eyed Mom's stomach and said, "I can't believe we came out of you."

I can't believe my family's idea of appropriate chitchat!!

I tilted my ice cream cone toward Mom, and she took a bite and thanked me. "This is heaven," she said. "Walking with you three on this beautiful night!"

It *was* beautiful. No stars, of course. The only time I saw the Big Dipper in New York City was during a blackout. Tonight's moon, however, was big and bright and round and romantic.

I started thinking about Justin. Then Miguel. Then Justin. Then Miguel. Then I ordered myself to stop thinking about either of them!

Meanwhile, my family was continuing the debate

about what to do with Miguel—which bites to take of the Big Apple or *La Gran Manzana* (La Grahn Mon Son Ah).

"We could take a helicopter ride!" Matt suggested.

"Only if we rob a bank first," Dad said.

I can't believe Miguel arrives in less than a week!!! The anticipation is killing me. (Not literally. I take it back!)

Superstitiously,
Manzana Mel

Saturday June 16
2:00 P.M.

Dear Diary,

This morning, Dad started listening to an opera that's over five hours long. Since he's still acting depressed about turning forty on June 30, Mom did not want to say, "No! Please! Spare us! Not *Die Meistersinger!*" She likes opera—but not thaaaaat much.

She decided to take Matt and me out for Chinese food at Ollie's.

While Little Science Boy was dissecting the insides

of his egg roll with chopsticks, I sat up straight, got really really really brave, and announced, "Mom, I want to go back to Morris Bros."

"You want another top?"

I looked at her, shook my head, and mouthed: "I want a bra."

Out loud Mom said, "A what?"

I frowned, tilted my head toward Matt, made the *shhh* sign with my finger, pointed to my lower neck area, and repeated silently, "A bra!"

"Oh!" Mom said, her eyes wide. "Oh! Well! Okay!" She was doing a terrible job of acting normal. Of course, as soon as she figured it all out, I realized I should have picked a time to shop when it was just Mom and me—or just Cecily and me—but not Mom, me, and Tagalong Boy.

Too late. And before we even crossed the street and went into the store, Matt started whining, "You said lunch! You didn't say shopping!"

"We'll be quick," Mom said, and I ducked straight into the changing room in the back while Matt ran up and down the stairs. Mom started handing me bras, and I started trying them on. I didn't want Mom or the saleslady to come in, but I'm not exactly a bra expert (a B.E.?), so how was I supposed to know if they fit?

Imagine trying shoes on for the first time in your whole entire life. Would you think, "Wow, these are comfortable!"? No, because barefoot is more comfortable. But you *need* shoes.

Well, I felt I needed a bra. Whether I need need need one or not (if you know what I mean).

I kept asking Mom, "Are there any other kinds?" She kept pushing more and more over the top of the changing-room door. Small ones and big ones and ones with adjustable straps and ones with no straps at all and ones that squashed into nothing and ones with soft padding. It was much more complicated than I thought!

I will say this: I checked the store mirror, and I liked the way I looked with a bra on. I looked older. More grown-up. More mature.

Dad's worried about getting old, but I've been worrying about staying young. And getting left behind.

For a while I wanted everything to stay the same, but nothing was—except me.

I keep staying the same up top, which is frustrating, but I can't do anything about that. Except wait. Well, today over lunch, I realized that I *could* at least control whether I'd be wearing undershirts for the rest of my life.

Outside the changing room, I heard Matt, who had been racing all over the store, suddenly stomp up and complain, "What's taking so long?"

"Melanie is trying things on," Mom said, which was nice and discreet of her.

"Mel! Hurry up!! Or just come out and we'll tell you if you look dorky." Neither Mom nor I said anything. "What's she trying on, anyway?"

"Shoes!" I yelled, which was stupid because that's the one thing Morris Bros. doesn't sell.

"Whoa!" Matt suddenly gasped. "Is that what I think it is? Is that a bra???" I wished he hadn't figured it out. I knew I should have waited to go shopping alone with Mom—but I didn't know when I'd feel brave again. "Melanie wears a BRA?" Matt asked the entire store. "I didn't even know she had BOOBIES!"

"Matt, you are so dead!" I said. "Mom, shut him up NOW!"

"Matthew, be quiet," Mom scolded.

I looked in the dressing-room mirror, and instead of the pretty almost-teenager who'd been right there a second ago, there was this dumb, flat-chested kid with a bra strapped on her.

Mom was whispering furiously, and Matt was saying, "Okay, okay." Then he said, "I'm sorry, Melanie. You can wear a bra if you want to."

"Thanks for your permission!" I put my clothes back on and stormed out of the dressing room.

"C'mon, don't be mad, Mel. I think of you as my sister. Not as a *girl*."

"Well, I think of you as a stupid little idiot. You act like you have no I.Q."

Without meeting Mom's eyes, I handed her three bras and said, "These." Then, even though Matt *is* a stupid little I.Q.-less idiot, I said, "Come outside," because one thing for sure, I was *not* going to stay inside and stand there watching a cashier ring up my bras!

Matt and I waited on Broadway, and Mom came out with the shopping bag. A big part of me was embarrassed, but another big part was happy. I like hand-me-downs, but I wanted brand-new bras. And now I have three. One white. One beige. One pink.

And they're mine mine mine.

Mission accomplished!

Back home, Dad was *still* listening to his opera. Those singers have been *la la la*ing all day! Is this Dad's idea of a good time, or is he torturing us on purpose, or is he wallowing in Wagner because he's in a bad mood about his birthday?

When will it end? (The bad mood and the opera!)

La La La —
Melanie the BRAVE

P.S. The word "brave" has the word "bra" buried in it—which is probably a weird thing to notice!!

thirty minutes later

I just changed and I'm wearing my white bra. I have to keep pulling on it. But it feels okay, I guess.

Cecily is coming soon for a sleepover. YAY!! I hope the opera singers will be done by the time she gets here.

Next week, Cecily is going on vacation with her dad. Which means she won't meet Miguel. Which is too bad.

Tonight she said she'd bring her Amsterdam T-shirt, the one that matches mine. She'll also bring Snow Bear and her three-inch square of worn-out baby blanket that her Grandma Flo knitted for her. Am I still the only one besides her parents who knows about that scrap of blankie? Maybe Suze knows too. I hope not.

It's funny how Cecily and I both have bras but still have stuffies. I hope I never outgrow Hedgehog!

6/17 4ish
at Mom's hair salon

Dear Diary,

In Spanish, *me siento* (May Syen Toe) means "I sit" and also "I feel." Since I'm stuck here waiting for Mom, I'm going to sit and tell you how I feel.

I don't like being called "tween" or "preteen." But I do like that sixth graders are in middle school and are in the middle of being kids and teenagers. Last night Cecily and I gave ourselves makeovers and took pictures of ourselves posing like models and laughing.

Is every age a little mixed-up?

People my age try to look older, but people my parents' age try to look younger!

I'm now in a chair in a corner of Mom's hair salon, waiting for her to get her hair colored, rinsed, and blow-dried. The whole place is filled with young people trying to help not-young people look young again.

Mom is reading, but I can see her in the mirror. She has goo and a showercappy thing on her head, and she looks reeeeally bad, a total BEFORE.

Mom used to have a little gray in her hair. Now it's pure brown. This is how she puts it: "I used to be salt and pepper, but now I'm chestnuts and chocolate." She laughs when she says that, but is it funny?

Well, I'm getting older, so obviously Dad and Mom are too.

Will I ever look like Mom looks now?

Will I ever want to look younger?

What *is* the perfect age?

Maybe there is no perfect age since there's no perfect anything.

Anyway, I'm changing the subject because you can do that in a diary. In fact, a diary is the perfect place for random thoughts.

Here's one. Miguel comes tomorrow, and lately it's been as if different parts of New York have been auditioning for me.

For instance, Mom and I got out of the subway at Columbus Circle, and I swear it was as if Columbus himself called out, "Hey, kid, look up! Your friends see me but you never look!" So I looked and it's true: I'd never before noticed him standing proud on his column decorated with anchors.

I like to think I'm observant, but in New York, there's so much to observe!

Today I also observed American flags flapping and fluttering on schools, museums, hotels, and post offices. How come I'd never noticed?

The building at 9 West 57th Street is not a regular rectangle but a giant gentle slide. A cartoon character could skateboard down it! How come I'd never noticed that either?

On the same street, there's a whole entire row of clocks with city names above them, like Paris and Tokyo and Moscow, so you can tell what time it is around the world. I'd never stopped to look.

NEW YORK

LONDON

PARIS

Well, I looked, and even though Valencia was not up there, I knew it was evening in Spain. So I whispered into the sky, "*Hasta mañana* (Ah Sta Mon Yon Ah), Miguel! See you tomorrow!"

I wonder if I'll see more new things once I'm with him.

I wonder how it will feel to see *him*.

Wonderingly,

Melanie in the Middle

Dear Diary,

Miguel's plane is about to land!

I'm excited but also nervous or *nerviosa* (Nare V O Sa). I tried on about ten outfits—and put back all the rejects.

Mom is not nervous, but she was three months ago when she was about to see Antonio, her old boyfriend, after a long time apart.

She's been doing one of her big summertime puzzles. Mom says that in Spanish, puzzles are called *rompecabezas*, or Rrrome Pay Ca Bay Soss, which means head breakers, but you can also say *puzzle*, or Pooz Lay. Mom's pooz lay is of a painting by a New Yorker named Edward Hopper. I don't know why Mom likes him. The people in his paintings all seem lonely. Even when they're not alone.

Matt and I have been trying to help Mom find and connect edge pieces. I found way more than Matt. But it was hard. Sometimes a piece looks just right, but you can never be sure that it fits until you try it.

Mom just checked Miguel's flight and it's on time, so we're about to pick him and his uncle up at JFK! We usually tell visitors to take a taxi. But our visitors usually speak excellent English. Dad's coming too—he's leaving work early.

I can't believe Miguel is almost here!!!

I hope we'll be able to pick up where we left off. Of course, where we left off was with his giving me a kiss.

Is it *my* turn to give *him* a kiss? Shoud I?

Where??? HOW ????

When??

Breathlessly,

Mlni (that's Melanie with no breeeaaath)

in the CAR

I just realized that I didn't put my fan necklace back on! How could I have forgotten?? I hope Miguel doesn't notice. But I bet he will! Shoot shoot shoot! I'm so mad at myself!

I hope I can tell him with just my eyes 👁 👁 that I still like him more than other guys.

Dear Diary,

We are waiting for a plane.

I am trying to stay sane.

It's lucky it is a clear clear clear day, because once they get here, we're going to take Miguel and Uncle Angel (Antonio's younger brother) up the Empire State Building.

I've gone up only one time. Matt says he never has, but Mom and Dad said he did as a baby in a Snugli—they have photos. Matt said that doesn't count, and Dad admitted that going up is the kind of thing New Yorkers do with out-of-towners. Mom added, "Which is one reason why it's fun to have visitors."

It's 4:10. I wish time would hurry up!

I just went to the bathroom. The floor is made of little squares and the wall is made of medium squares and the ceiling is made of big squares. The bathroom mirror is like the school's mirror, meaning I looked disgusting in it. I hope it was because of bad lighting!

"Matt," I asked, "do I look okay?"

"No. But you never look okay."

121

He probably expected me to punch him, but I didn't. Maybe I looked sad because he quickly added, "Mellie, you look fine. I like your shirt."

Matt never notices my shirts, so I said, *"Gracias."*

He smiled and said, *"De nada"* (Day Na Da).

When will Miguel get here???

He and Uncle Angel had to fly from Valencia to Barcelona, so they've had a long travel day. Even though Uncle Angel let us stay in his apartment when we were in Spain, Mom hasn't actually seen him in seventeen years. She pronounces his name On Hell (!) and said to look for a skinny man with a big halo of dark hair.

We're looking!

I just checked the TV monitor. For a while, it said: Barcelona On Time. Then it switched to Barcelona In Range. Now it says Barcelona Arrived.

You'd think it would say: Barcelona Arrived!!!!!!!!! Yippee! Yippee! Yippee! Woo-Hoo! Woo-Hoo! Woo-Hoo!

People are coming through the automatic sliding doors! No Miguel and no Angel-with-a-Halo, though. Maybe they're going through Customs?

Dad called out to one man, "Barcelona?" but he answered, "Budapest." Mom asked a lady, "Barcelona?" but she said, "Cairo."

More and more people are pouring through!

New York City is popular! Which seems strange. I mean, I just think of it as home.

I keep looking up and not seeing Miguel or his uncle. I hope they don't walk in while I'm writing. What if Miguel arrives while I'm looking down instead of up?

I better put you away.

Looking Up,
Melanie

P.S.

I hope our visit will go well.
Until it starts, it's hard to tell.

10:30 P.M. in (bed)

Dear Diary,

He's here!!! They arrived!!!

At the airport, a lot of Americans gave each other big back-slapping hugs, but Miguel and Uncle Angel gave us little Spanish cheek kisses.

Uncle Angel, by the way, does *not* have a hair halo. He has no hair at all! He's bald! He's not skinny either. He's the opposite! He's nice but his English is only okay. He pronounces Dad's name Maaaarrrrrc and Mom's Me Ron Dah and mine May Lah Nee. And he calls New York *Nueva York* (Nway Va Yohrrk).

Miguel looks the same: cute. But is he maybe a little shorter? That makes no sense, of course. Unless I grew a little. Which I'm sure I did. But did I also imagine him taller? Another thing (I can't believe I'm writing this): His shoes are a tiny bit unusual. I mean, no boy in my class would ever wear loafers like his.

Anyway, we put their stuff (or "luggages," as Uncle Angel said) in our trunk and Uncle Angel smoked a cigarette (yuk!) and then we drove from JFK to NYC.

124

From the Triborough Bridge, Mom pointed out the changing Manhattan skyline.

"Look at the Empire State Building!" she said. We all turned our heads—even Dad—and admired how the Empire State Building sparkled, all rosy and golden and dramatic in the sunshine. But then Mom scolded, "Not you, Sweetheart, you drive!"

Uncle Angel said, "It is beauty-full!"

"Want to go up?" Dad asked.

Uncle Angel said, "Yace!" It was fun to see a grown-up so excited. This is *his* first trip to *Nueva York* too, not just Miguel's.

Dad told them that on the Fourth of July, America's birthday, the top part gets lighted up all red, white, and blue.

"On Saint Patrick's Day, it's green," Matt said.

"At Christmastime, it's red and green," I said.

"On Valentine's Day, it's just red," Mom said.

"And wasn't it bright blue when blue M&M's first came out?" Matt asked. I don't know where Matt learned that, but it was better than dwelling on Valentine's Day.

"It was also blue," Dad added, "when the Yankees won the World Series."

Miguel translated for his uncle. *"Los yanquis"* (Yon Keys). *"Béisbol"* (Baze Bowl). I knew those words because we'd studied sports in Spanish. I remember because Justin thought the word for outfielder was funny; it's *jardinero* (Hhhar D Nair Oh), which also means . . . gardener! In Spain, of course, no one actually plays baseball—it's an American game. (Random question: Does that mean Spanish couples never go to *first base*???)

Well, we drove down Fifth Avenue to 34th Street and our only choice was to park in an expensive garage. Uncle Angel seemed shocked at the price and said it cost *"Un ojo de la cara"* (Oon Oh Hho Day La Cah Rah). Mom translated: "An eye from the face."

"Ewww!" Matt squealed with delight.

Miguel gave Matt a big smile, the kind of smile I hoped he'd give me.

Matt said, "I can jump higher than the Empire State Building!"

Miguel said, "Is this possible?"

Matt said, "Yes, because the Empire State Building can't jump!"

Miguel laughed, so I did too.

We walked under the Empire State Building awning, and Miguel and Uncle Angel handed Dad their cameras, and Dad took photos of them pointing up. Inside the marble lobby, we looked at the Art Deco mural and got in a twisty line of tourists speaking different languages.

Dad mumbled, "We should have ordered tickets online."

Mom shrugged. "Lines are part of the New York Experience."

Our turn came, and Dad bought tickets for the observation deck and Tony's Audio Tour, a headset that Dad said would give us "an overview of the view."

Uncle Angel nodded. "An overview of the view. *Sí.*"

Well, Miguel and his uncle were blown away by the elevator ride alone! Elevators usually show floor numbers like 1, 2, 3 . . . but this elevator zoomed up so fast that the numbers it showed were 10, 20, 30 . . . ! My ears felt as if they were on an airplane! We rocketed to the 80th floor, then took another elevator to the 86th floor, which is the best for looking around. There are actually 102 stories and a giant antenna.

Uncle Angel asked, "We see King Kong?" Mom laughed and told us about an ancient movie that shows King Kong on the tippy top of the Empire State Building.

Finally we arrived at the observation deck, and we all looked out out out and saw, not King Kong, but the whole world at our feet. In miniature!

> From the observation deck,
> Even a taxi looks like a speck.

Miguel gasped. "It *is* like the movies, May Lah Nee!"

"It is!" I agreed. His eyes were wide, and I looked into them and we smiled at each other—at last! For one endless second, it felt like we were on our own private magic-carpet ride. Together, just us. I even wondered if I should give him that kiss I'd been thinking about.

Up there, it was as if everything else was fuzzy and only Miguel was in focus. His dark eyes and dark hair and soft lips. It seemed like we might step closer to-gether…but then we broke away. Maybe we both feel a little shy or *tímido* (T Me Dough)? Instead of gazing at each other, we started looking outward, and also down at the colorful metal panels that explain all the sites.

I pointed to the giant green rectangle of Central Park

and the pointy scalloped spire of the Chrysler Building and the graceful distant arch of the George Washington Bridge, which got built in 1931—same year as the Empire State Building. We looked at the toylike trees and itty-bitty Staten Island Ferries and teeny tiny Statue of Liberty (we put quarters in a viewer so we could see her better).

Miguel asked where the twin towers used to be, and I showed him. I also showed him how they are marked on the panels with dotted black lines.

The Empire State Building got built really fast—in fourteen months!! When it was done, it was the tallest building in the world. It stayed the tallest in New York all the way until 1972, when the World Trade Center became the tallest. Then everything changed on September 11, 2001, and the Empire State Building became the tallest again. But it wasn't really a boast anymore. More like a tarnished trophy.

Miguel looked toward the place that got named Ground Zero, or Zone Zero, as he put it. "*Terrorismo* (Tear Rrroar Ease Mo). Terrorism. It is sickening, yes?"

"Yes," I agreed, but then I couldn't think of a single

other thing to say. How come it was so much easier to write to Miguel than to talk to him?

Stupid Suze hopped into my head and answered, "Because you weren't in love, you were obsessed." Which made me mad at her even though she wasn't even there.

I think I'm just not used to discussing such serious subjects. Plus, I wanted to feel like a kid on top of the world—not a grown-up who knows that the world has troubles of its own.

Miguel and I turned on our audio guides. I listened in English and he listened in Spanish. Matt tagged along and started climbing a railing—until a guard yelled at him. Then Matt taught Miguel the phrase Never Eat Shredded Wheat, since that's how he'd learned North, East, South, and West. I told him that was dumb.

The Audio Tour was *not* dumb. We liked it! It starts with: "How ya doin'?" in a New Yawk accent. The guide, Tony, is a friendly, know-it-all taxi driver. He says the Empire State Building is the "greatest building" in the "greatest city in the world," then tells the history of New York, explaining sites from the Flatiron

Building (a really cool triangular building) to the dock where the *Titanic* was supposed to arrive (sad sad sad).

I wish I could have memorized everything Tony said; I wish I could be a five-star tour guide!

We went to the gift shop and Miguel bought a souvenir mug that cost exactly $10. The cashier said, "All set?" Miguel looked confused. She said, "Cash or plastic?" Miguel looked more confused. Finally she said, "$10.70," and Miguel said, "Is there a confusion?" Mom explained that everything costs extra because of tax, and Dad added, "Welcome to America."

Miguel gave the cashier eleven dollars and she gave him change and Matt explained that a nickel is five cents and a quarter is twenty-five.

The elevator to the bottom was very crowded and Dad joked, "If we squeeze in a few more people, we can go down even faster!" Fortunately, Mom did not translate. I was squooshed against Miguel (which I didn't mind) and my ears were popping (which I did). Back on the street, Uncle Angel thanked us for a wonderful experience but said he was *hecho polvo* (Ay Cho Pole Vo). That means so tired he'd turned to dust. It was past midnight in Spain, so we dropped both Uncle Angel and Miguel at their hotel and went back to being just the four M's.

Which felt . . . disappointing. I don't know exactly what I'd expected—maybe that Miguel would be staying with us? Or that he would take a picture of me with him on the Empire State Building as he had on the castle in Segovia? Or that he'd kiss me on the forehead as he had in the airport in Madrid?? Or that I'd be brave and kiss him???

I guess things with Miguel are still up in the air. Which is where he spent most of his day!

At least he's on my side of the Atlantic. For now, anyway!

Back on Earth,
May Lah Nee

P.S. When Cecily and I talked about IMing, I'd said things are clearer when you're actually with someone, person to person. But even face to face, things can feel foggy.

I wish I could read Miguel's mind
But would I like what I would find?

June 19, 9:30 A.M.

just waking up

Dear Diary,

At around eleven last night, Dad brought me warm milk and asked, "Are you too wound up to wind down?"

I said, "Yes, but that's a dorky way to put it." I didn't want to tell him what (or who) I was wound up about, though he could probably guess.

I still can't believe Miguel is here!

This morning, Dad already went to work and Uncle Angel has meetings, so Mom, Matt, and I are going to show Miguel around.

I wish I were old enough to do it myself. I wonder if he wishes that too.

NOT OLD ENOUGH,
Melanie

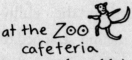
at the Zoo
cafeteria

(everyone's in line and my job is to save the table)

Dear Diary,

The Central Park Zoo is tiny compared to the Bronx Zoo, but Miguel thinks it's cool that there are monkeys right in the middle of busy Manhattan.

In Spanish, zoo is spelled *zoo* but rhymes with Toe.

Monkey is *mono* (Mo No). *Mono* also means cute. So if you're looking at monkeys and say, "*Mira, qué monos*" (Me Ra Kay Mo Nohs), it means two things: "Look! What monkeys!" and "Look! How cute!"

Miguel called Matt a "*mono mono*" and Matt beamed. If I'd called Matt a cute monkey, he'd have bit me.

Besides the monkeys, we watched:

• polar bears or *osos polares* (Oh Sose Po Lar S) swim, flip, and push off from the thick glassy wall with their big white paws.

• seals or *focas* (Foe Cahs) wave, clap, salute, bark, and give high fives for fishy rewards.

• penguins or *pingüinos* (Peen Gween Ohs) waddle

135

around their chilly stinky habitat making clicky noises in chin-strapped tuxedos. A few rubbed their necks together and sort of kissed with their beaks, which made me wonder:

ARE BEAK KISSES
LIKE CHEEK KISSES?

We also liked the flying bats or *murciélagos* (Moor Syell Ug Ose). Miguel told Mom that "bat" in Spanish is the only word that uses every vowel—aeiou—once each. Believe it or not, that made Mom's day.

Oops, everyone is back with lemonade or *limonada* (Lee Moan Ah Da).

Zoologically yours,
Melanie

P.S. Matt just asked Miguel, "Where do bats go to pee?" "Where?" Miguel asked. "The bat room!" Matt howled. "Come with me, okay?"

Off they've now gone to the bat room, ho ho ho, Matt babbling the whole way about how a little brown bat can eat one thousand bugs in an hour.

I wish I could talk with Miguel the way my family does. Matt made Miguel laugh just by telling him that elbows in English are called funny bones. Miguel asked, "And knees?" Matt said, "Knees are just knees!" and they laughed some more. Ha ha ha ho ho ho. Everything is soooo funny.

All I wanted was for things with Miguel not to change. But even Miguel's voice is changing. It's deeper, and it cracks sometimes.

I guess I'm changing too. I'm taller, and today I'm wearing a bra. It's a little uncomfortable, though.

Dear Diary,

Outside the zoo, a small crowd of people gathered, and we joined them and looked up toward a brick archway. Music filled the air, and bronze animals started moving in a circle. A penguin played a drum; kangaroos played horns; an elephant played the accordion; a bear banged a tambourine; a hippo played the violin; and on top, two monkeys rang a big bell.

"*Mono*," Monkey Boy said, since he's proud of his new word.

"This is . . . ?" Miguel asked.

"The Delacorte Clock," Mom said. "It does this every half hour. When Matt was in a stroller and Mel was in pigtails, they adored this clock."

"Pigtails?" Miguel asked.

I shot Mom a look that said: "Please don't explain!" Too late. She'd already picked up her hair in two high bunches.

Sometimes she doesn't get it! After Spring Fling, she met Justin and said, "I've heard a lot about you," when it would have been much better not to say anything!!

138

Miguel smiled and said, "I like it. *Me gusta*" (May Goo Stah). I wasn't sure if he meant the clock or the pigtails.

We left the zoo and walked south, past artists drawing flattering charcoal portraits of tourists, artists drawing insulting caricatures of tourists, people selling I ♡ NY shirts to tourists, and horse-drawn carriages giving rides to tourists.

Who knew New York was so STUFFED with tourists?

An old black horse made me think of Black Beauty. I looked at Mom and whispered, "Carriage ride?" She whispered, "Too expensive." (No surprise.) So we just watched carriages clip-clop by. One had a couple in it, but they weren't being very couple-y. The man was taking photos of the park on his side, and the woman was taking a video of the park on her side.

Next stop: the Plaza. We went up the red carpet, held on to the gold stair rail, pushed through the revolving door, and walked under the big chandelier to the Palm Court, where dressed-up people can have tea and listen to harp music. I showed Miguel the big painting of Eloise, who lived at the Plaza with Nanny; her dog, Weenie; and her turtle, Skipperdee. I love Eloise, but

Miguel didn't even know who she was. You can be famous in one country and unknown in another! Even though it was a little embarrassing, everyone had to wait for me to go to the Plaza's bathroom, since I'd been writing when I was supposed to have gone at the zoo. (I prefer fancy bathrooms anyway!)

Next we crossed Fifth Avenue, passed the FAO Schwartz clock, and headed north. Mom and Matt were walking ahead, and Miguel and I were behind. I wanted to say something deep or romantic, but somehow I started telling him about how Cecily's cat likes to bite the end of toilet paper rolls, then race through the apartment with tp flying behind him. I also told him about how Cheshire once licked some water—but it was *sparkling* water—and it made him sneeze sneeze sneeze!

My stories made Miguel laugh, and that felt good.

Mom smiled at us and said, "I hope your shoes are comfortable, Miguel, because in New York, everyone gets lots of exercise without even trying."

At the corner of East 70th Street, we reached a mansion that used to belong to a rich guy named Frick. Mom took me once last fall. The Frick is loaded with masterpieces, but it's small—so it's not overwhelming like the Met. The problem? You have to be *ten* to be allowed in.

When Mom planned Miguel's day, she forgot that Monkey Boy is not even eight!

"What are we going to do?" I asked.

"Have a hot dog?" Matt suggested.

Mom bought us hot dogs from a hot dog man under an umbrella. I got mine with ketchup; Miguel did too. I think he was a little surprised that we ate them standing up—Spanish lunches are often two-course (or even three-course) sit-down meals.

*When you have lunch in New York,
you don't always need a fork.* 🍴

"*Delicioso*" (Day Lee See Oh So), Miguel said, and Mom offered him another one. He accepted and asked, "You know how we say 'hot dog'?" I shook my head. "Hot puppy! *¡Perrito caliente!*" (Pair E Toe Cahl E N Tay). Matt cracked up. "And you know how we say 'children' in slang?"

"*¿Niños?*" (Nee Nyose), I asked.

"*Mocosos* (Mo Co Sohs). It means 'Snotty noses.'"

"Ewwwwwww!" Matt shouted, happy as can be.

A lady with long legs followed by a puppy with short legs scowled at Matt as though he were a problem child—which, of course, he is.

Mom looked worried. "Matt, listen carefully. Can you pretend to be ten?"

"*Sí,*" Matt said.

"No monkey business," Mom added.

"But I'm a *mono mono!*" Matt started scratching his armpits and ooh-ooh-oohing.

"I need you to be a serious boy," Mom said. "We'll stay just a few minutes, but I'd hate for Miguel to miss

142

the Frick. It has three Vermeers!" To us, she added, "I hope Matt doesn't get ants in his pants."

Miguel looked alarmed. "Ants?"

Mom laughed. "It's an expression! It means: I hope he doesn't get restless—antsy."

Inside, she showed her membership card, and the man asked how old we were. Mom said, "Twelve, eleven, and ten." He eyed Matt suspiciously, but Matt flashed his Angel Boy Smile, and the man waved us in.

"Behave," Mom whispered again, and handed us Art-Phone audio guides. Miguel's was in *español* (S Pon Yole).

We walked through the peaceful courtyard with its trickling fountain, then entered the big room.

"The kids sometimes play a museum game," Mom started explaining. I nearly *died* because I didn't think Mom even knew about Point Out the Naked People.

"A game?" Miguel said.

"Yes. Sometimes I ask them, 'If you could have one painting in this room, which would you choose?'" Oh, *phew! That* museum game! "Everyone walks around, then we meet in the middle, and I say, 'One two three,' and we all point to our favorite."

"Let's play," Matt said.

"Ready?" Mom said.

We walked around, then met in the middle. "All right," Mom said. *"Uno dos tres."*

We were pointing in different directions, and I said, "You go first, Mom."

"I love the Rembrandt self-portrait." We walked over to it.

"You're supposed to say why," I said.

"Because he looks kind and real and sad and wise."

"If you could save only one painting in the whole world, would this be the one?" Matt asked.

"What would happen to the others?" Mom said.

"I don't know. Fire? A flood? Turpentine?"

She looked pained, so Matt changed the question. "I just mean: Is this your top favorite painting of all time?"

"I think so." Mom turned to Miguel and said, "Doesn't Rembrandt have a wonderful face? I always say hello to him when I come here. I like to think of him as an old friend. Maybe a grandfather."

Grandpa Rembrandt.

I looked to see if Miguel thought Mom was crazy—
loca (Low Cah)—but he just smiled. Mom continued,
"I like to think he's saying, 'And what have you been
up to since you last came to see me?'" She laughed.
"Okay, someone else's turn. Matt, you go."

Matt said, "Same as Mom."

"Copycat!" I rolled my eyes. "How about you, Miguel?"

"I have picked *Felipe IV*" (Fay Leap Ay Qua Tro).

"Velázquez's *Philip IV*," Mom said. "Why?"

"I like seeing our king in your country." Maybe since
Mom is an art teacher, Miguel added, "And I like the gold
in his cloak and the orange in his hair."

I gave Miguel a smile and I think he winked. But
maybe it was just a funny blink? I wanted to ask him,
but then I realized that you can't ask a boy if he winked
at you or not.

"And you, May Lah Nee?" Miguel asked. For a second, I started picturing myself giving him a little kiss
right then and there, but of course I had nowhere near
enough guts. Besides, we were with my *family*!

"Your turn, Mel!" Matt said, which yanked me out of
my daydream.

I said, "Georges de La Tour." We walked over, and I said I liked how the candlelight was reflected in the girl's, Mary's, face, and how the light coming through her fingers turned them see-through, like when you shine a flashlight behind your hand. Then I noticed its title, *The Education of the Virgin*. I did *not* want Miguel to read that, so I said, "Let's keep going!"

Mom said, "Shall we go to the Fragonard Room to see *The Progress of Love?*"

"No!!" I said too loudly, since that title was even worse.

Miguel said, "It is very tranquil here."

"No Snotty Noses," I agreed.

Right on cue, Matt bounded over, looked up and down the long hallway, and said, "Mom, you'd kill me if I ran back and forth, right?"

"Correct," she said. "So you'd end up dead and I'd end up in jail. Don't do it, okay?"

"Okay," Matt said.

"Slow down and let the paintings speak to you."

"Okay," Matt said. Then he whispered to me, "Naked Statue Alert," and pointed out some R-rated sculptures on the long table behind us.

146

Mom sighed and led us to the room with the George Washington painting.

"Can I sit down?" Matt asked, eyeing an ancient embroidered chair.

"Don't you dare!" Mom practically shouted. "In fact, we'd better go—though I hate to rush you, Miguel."

"I don't mind to leave," Miguel said. "A skyscratcher, a zoo, a hotel of luxury, a museum—I have already seen a lot of New York."

"We're just getting started!" Mom said, adding that *rascacielos* (Ra Ska Syell Ohse) is skyscraper not skyscratcher.

We were about to go when Matt pointed out the window by the coat check and shouted, "Baby ducks!" He started hollering, "Melanie!! Miguel!!" until I whispered, "Matt, you're *ten*."

"Oh yeah. I forgot."

I looked out the window and saw a little pond with goldfish and lily pads and purple and white flowers, but no ducks.

Suddenly I saw the ducklings too, and they were *adorable* (Odd Or Ob Lay). "*¡Pato!*" (Pa Toe), I said, and pointed at one.

"Patitos" (Pa Tee Toes), Miguel replied. He was behind me, and he held my pointing hand in his hand and moved it from duckling to duckling, and we counted together in Spanish. There were eight or *ocho* (Oh Cho). I wish there had been eighty!!! I liked the way his hand felt holding mine up.

He touched my hand,
and and and—
it felt good.
(I thought it would!)

Soon other people came over to see what we were staring at. Before long, there were more people oohing and aahing at the ducklings than had been oohing and aahing at the paintings. The baby ducks followed their mom everywhere, hopping over and scooting under the lily pads.

"Vámonos" (Ba Moan Ohs), Mom said, which means "Let's go." She suggested we walk across Central Park, and I couldn't object since I'd sent Miguel that Nature Girl e-mail.

Mom must have read my mind, because she said, "A little sunshine will feel good and will help Miguel get over jet lag. Once we get to the West Side, we'll take a taxi. Deal?" I nodded.

Central Park is giant. You could walk all day and not see it all. It goes from the East Side (Fifth Avenue) to the West Side (Central Park West). And from 59th Street all the way up to 110th.

We walked and walked (well, Matt also skipped), and Miguel liked how people on horseback trotted by and how teams of kids were playing sports and how a few mothers were jogging with babies in special strollers and how we were in a park but surrounded by tall buildings. The grass in one area was freshly cut, and Matt said it smelled "green," and I said *"verde"* (Bear Day), and we all talked about whether colors have smells. We passed Bethesda Terrace and got to Strawberry Fields. Miguel said, "Strawberry? *Fresa?*" (Fray Sa).

Mom started singing the Beatles song (she never gets embarrassed!), then pointed out the Dakota, the building where John Lennon was killed in 1980. She explained that his widow, Yoko Ono, gave a million dollars and got lots of different countries to send plants and help make a Garden of Peace.

Miguel took a photo of the black-and-white mosaic that says IMAGINE, and Mom started singing that song too. "Imagine all the people, living life in peace . . ."

Suddenly a squirrel dashed out and Miguel shouted, "¡Ardilla!" (R D Ya). I said that squirrels are totally common here, no big deal, but Miguel didn't care. It was as if he had seen an endangered rhinoceros or something. He took more photos of the squirrel than he'd taken of the penguins or polar bears or monkeys or me. Combined! He even asked me to take one of him in front of a tree with a squirrel climbing up the trunk. Which I did, but I was a teeny tiny bit annoyed because I'd never been upstaged by a bushy-tailed squirrel before.

If I had pointed at the squirrel, would Miguel have taken my hand and helped me count all the squirrels in the park?

Instead of passing Tavern on the Green, we walked north to the theater where Shakespeare plays are performed outdoors in the summer. There's a statue of

Romeo and Juliet, and Juliet's head is tilted up, and her hair is falling straight down behind her, and she's on tiptoe, and she and Romeo are almost (but not quite) kissing. I don't think Miguel noticed it, but I did:

A near kiss?
A near miss?

Will Miguel and I kiss again?

When he was far away, I missed him soooo much. But now, even though he's right here, it's as if I still miss him a tiny bit. What is there between us, now that the Atlantic Ocean isn't between us? Do girls usually think about love and stuff more than boys? And did I imagine Miguel as too good to be true? In Spain, he seemed to know about everything, but here there's so much he doesn't know about—like squirrels! Maybe when you're on vacation, everything and everyone seems extra wonderful? When Miguel went to Galicia, even he described rain as magic mist, not gloppy drops. Does everything depend on how you look at it?

Back home, we showed Miguel our many mice and one little fish, Wanda. My bedroom was a mess, so I closed the door, but Matt proudly showed Miguel his room—and new bullfighter poster.

Speaking of posters, I'm glad I remembered to take down my sketches from the closet doors, a.k.a. Mom's Art Gallery. Matt's dorky doodles are up on display, along with postcards of real art. Mom could have been a curator. (That's the word for a person who arranges museum shows.) Right now she has a bunch of postcards up. She calls it her "American Exhibit."

Miguel complimented Matt's pitiful sketches and looked at the American flags by Jasper Johns, bones by Georgia O'Keeffe, farmers with a pitchfork by Grant Wood, soup cans by Andy Warhol, and cowboys by Frederic Remington.

"Cowboys!" Miguel said. "We learned about them in school." He looked closely at a painting by Norman Rockwell of ten happy people and an old lady serving a giant turkey. "Thanksgiving. We studied this too."

It seemed funny to study stuff we take for granted.

"Did you learn about Harriet Tubman?" I asked, pointing to a Jacob Lawrence postcard. He shook his head. "She helped slaves escape."

"We learned about slavery," Miguel assured me. He pointed to some Jackson Pollock splotches. "You like?"

"Not as much as these." I showed him a chubby baby by Mary Cassatt. He smiled and it was almost as if we were playing Mom's museum game, just the two of us.

"And this?" He pointed to a funny photograph by William Wegman of a dressed-up dog with an umbrella.

I laughed. "My mom has weird taste—in art." Since his dad and my mom had dated, I didn't want him to think I thought that she had weird taste in people.

I pointed to a country scene by Grandma Moses. "She was in her seventies when she began these oil paintings."

"Inspiring, yes?" He put his hand next to mine, and suddenly *we* were inspired and were showing each other the tiny trees and horses and children, our fingers almost touching.

Matt blurted out, "Miguel, come watch TV!" I wanted to bonk Matt on the head, but Miguel went toward the sofa and sat down. And conked out! Mom said it's tiring to talk another language all day, so it was good he was taking a catnap or *siesta* (Sea S Tah).

His *siesta* is also giving me a chance to catch up in you. When too much happens and I don't write it down, I get so full of words I feel as if I might burst.

Mom is next to me emptying the dishwasher. She just said, "Miguel is a nice young man."

I didn't disagree.

She probably wanted me to say more, but I stayed quiet.

We saw a lot lot lot today,
but I don't have much to say —
not to my mom anyway!

Yours with tired
and a tired
M.

P.S. Should I put the necklace Miguel gave me back on? Would that seem too obvious? Or would that be nice? Would he even notice??

Dear Diary,

a teeny bit later

I wrote another little poem.

> Miguel's siesta will soon end.
> I think he's more than just a friend.
> But how much does he care for me?
> I guess I'll have to wait and see.

I decided to put the necklace back on.

Fans open and close.

Maybe relationships do too.

 Metaphorically,
Mel

bedtime

Dear Diary,

Uncle Angel came over to pick up Miguel and to have dinner. Instead of cooking, we ordered in. Mom and Dad wished that they'd been able to cook an elaborate homemade meal, but I think Uncle Angel and Miguel got a kick out of seeing how New Yorkers sometimes make dinner.

They get out their menu file, make a decision, and make a phone call!

"Should we order in Indian?" Mom said.

"We don't speak Indian!" Matt said, because he loves that joke.

"Or Korean?" Dad asked. "Japanese? Vietnamese?"

"How about Malaysian?" Matt said.

"*¿En serio?*" (N Sare E O), Miguel asked. "Are you serious?"

"It's yummy!"

"I've never had Malaysian," Uncle Angel said.

"We could do Italian or Mexican or Cuban," Mom suggested.

"Any foods are okay," Uncle Angel said. "Don't molest yourself."

"What?!" Matt said, looking shocked.

Mom corrected Uncle Angel's English: "We say 'Don't *trouble* yourself,'" she said, then explained to us that *No se moleste* (No Say Mow Less Tay) is a common expression in Spanish.

We settled on Thai, Dad phoned in our order, and around fifteen minutes later, our doorman called to announce the delivery. Mom said, "Send him up." Uncle Angel was amazed.

Mom was looking for money for the dinner and tip; Dad was showing Uncle Angel our apartment; Miguel and I were setting the table; and Matt's job was to pour the milk.

Not a hard job, but obviously beyond him.

"Oh no!!!" Matt said.

Mom was in the doorway paying the delivery man. "What's the matter?"

"You know how you always say you'll love me no matter what?" Matt asked.

"What did you do?"

"And you know how everyone says, 'Don't cry over spilt milk?'"

"Matthew Martin, what are you trying to pull?"

"People shouldn't *yell* over spilt milk either." Matt scrunched up his face, hoping his adorableness would save him.

Mom looked at the kitchen floor and saw that he had dropped an *entire quart* of sticky chocolate milk on it. If Miguel and Uncle Angel hadn't been there, she might have exploded, but since they were, she just sighed, put down the brown bag of satay and spring rolls, and helped Matt mop up.

We lit candles, and it felt like a dinner party, even though it was take-in. I hope I'm a good host, because Miguel is a good guest—he kept refilling everyone else's water glasses and offering seconds to the rest of us before taking more himself. In Spanish and English, everyone talked about politics and Santiago Calatrava, a famous architect from Valencia who designed our World Trade Center PATH station. Mom also described Miguel's first full day here. She said he saw New York in a nutshell.

"Nutshell?" Miguel asked, looking handsome by candlelight.

Mom explained.

"Nooo Yorrrk een ay nutta shell!" Uncle Angel repeated, delighted.

Suddenly Miguel said, "The gift!" Uncle Angel dug into his bag and handed Mom a ceramic plate with Don Quixote on it. Mom said, "Thank you! Our whole family will enjoy this!" But I confess I wish he'd brought something just for me.

Uncle Angel smiled and got out a cigarette, which made us four M's stop smiling and start looking at each other. Dad said, "Mind not smoking inside?"

Uncle Angel looked surprised but said, "No, no. Clearly. Ees okay." He put away his cigarettes and got out his guidebook that explains New York. And we all planned our next tourist stop: Broadway.

Your host with the most
May Lah Nee Nee Nee

P.S. I wish I had a guidebook to explain Miguel. And Cecily. And maybe Justin too.

June 20 or *20 junio* (Who Knee Oh)

noonish

Dear Diary,

"What is that awful smell?" I heard Mom ask as I stepped out of the shower. Matt and I answered, "Mice" at the exact same time, then both yelled, "Jinx!"

The mouse cage needed cleaning (obviously), so Matt got out our dinky second cage and put shavings in it with the exercise wheel and an empty toilet paper roll. We temporarily transferred the mice, including the teenage ones and nine tiny new ones (Peanut, Butter, Hickory, Dickory, Dock, Sunshine, Snowball, Snowbell, and Speedy Gonzalez), into our second, smaller cage. After the transfer, Mom picked up the big mouseless cage, turned it upside down, and dumped its stinky shavings and pooplets into the giant trash can in a hallway outside our apartment.

Suddenly Matt burst into tears and said there were only EIGHT babies in the dinky cage instead of NINE! I panicked. Mom grumbled that cleaning the mouse cage shouldn't even be her job. But Matt was bawling, so she went back to the trash can and started sifting through the garbage in search of the missing mousie/mouseton/mouselet/mouseling.

It was pretty gross and Mom was pretty mad. Matt and I offered to help, but she said that since I had just showered and Matt had just taken a bath, there was no point in our getting dirty again. After another few minutes, she announced, "Matt, I'm not finding the mouse, and I don't think I threw it away. Could you take one more look in the small cage?"

Matt looked, and guess what? There, hidden inside the toilet paper roll, was Missing Mouse Baby #9, safe and sound. It was either Snowball or Snowbell; we're not sure. Matt was really happy. Me too. Mom was half happy, half annoyed.

Well, all's well that ends well!

I guess I shouldn't have gotten so so so worried—but that seems to be my specialty.

Your unworried friend,

Melanie of the Missing
            Mouse
        Mystery

Dear Diary,

"There ees no beeznees like show beeznees," Uncle Angel said, looking proud of himself. Matt high-fived him.

We were at a Broadway musical! Our seats were in the middle of the row, which meant we had a good view but also that we had to disturb a lot of people just to sit down.

The lights dimmed, and an announcement reminded people to turn off their cell phones and unwrap any crinkly candies. Matt whispered to Mom, "We should have brought candy! They expect you to!" Mom said, "Shhhh!"

Everyone shushed, the conductor waved his baton around, and hummable music sprung up from the sunken orchestra.

Uncle Angel and Miguel were both smiling—I peeked.

I was next to Miguel and we were sharing an armrest, but our arms never ended up resting at the same time. The armrest was actually too skinny for both of our arms.

Mom was happy that Miguel and Uncle Angel were getting to see a musical—and that we got half-price tickets. She wanted to take them to a classic like *West Side Story* or *Showboat* or *Guys and Dolls* or *Annie Get Your Gun*. But musicals open and close (like fans), so you have to pick from what's playing.

Well, I've heard of Great American Novels, like *To Kill a Mockingbird* and *Of Mice and Men*, but I'd never heard of Great American Musicals. Are there Great American Movies too? Maybe *E.T.* and *The Wizard of Oz*? (Random thought: E.T. kept wanting to phone home and Dorothy kept wanting to go home. I guess I'm glad I *am* home!)

ANYWAY, *Oklahoma!* was *perfecto* for Miguel and Uncle Angel because it had lots of singing, dancing, costumes, and scenery. Mom had to whisper a few explanations in Spanish to Uncle Angel—but she had to explain stuff in English to Matt too.

The most embarrassing song in *Oklahoma!* is about a boy-crazy girl who LOVES kissing. She thinks she should play hard-to-get, but she never does. She says she's just a girl who can't say no.

I don't think I play hard-to-get. I hope I don't play too easy-to-get. Do I play medium-to-get?

At the end of the musical, and the end of all the clapping, we went outside and Mom started humming, "OOOOOOKLAHOMA, where the wind comes sweepin' down the plain . . ." But the wind was sweeping around Times Square!

Miguel and Uncle Angel couldn't believe all the flashing colorful lights and enormous billboards and nonstop action. It felt as if we were surrounded by humongous TV sets, all high above our heads with different commercials on. A ring of moving words was giving headlines. A billboard for noodle soup had steam coming out. A billboard for Coke was supersized (Mom says too much soda makes people supersized). There were ads for plays and movies and bras and underpants. And you could buy deli sandwiches, popcorn, perfume, sunglasses, sweatshirts, incense, and hamburgers or *hamburguesas* (Ahm Booer Gay Soss). Miguel liked the Toys "R" Us store with the giant sixty-foot-high Ferris wheel inside it and the chocolate store with the giant, glittery Hershey's Kiss outside it.

Crowds of tourists were looking up, families were leaving theaters, couples were getting in and out of yellow cabs and white limousines, Uncle Angel and Miguel were taking pictures, and more and more people kept streaming out of the subway.

Matt and I played a new game he calls Tourist or New Yorker? Some tourists were easy to pick out because they had maps or name tags or they dressed funny or had matching T-shirts. But often, we couldn't tell who was who.

Tourists like looking at our town—
but we like looking them up and down!

Now I wonder if I stick out when I'm a tourist. Today I was half tourist, half tour guide. Could anyone tell?

Well, Dad met us and we all six went . . . underground! He led us down down down and through a turnstile and a bunch of wide tunnels like an endless rabbit hole. Mom held Matt's hand tight as we paused to watch Peruvian musicians playing flutes, a Latin man dancing to salsa music with a big rag doll, teenagers doing backflips and spinning around on the hard floor, and a woman with a guitar singing love songs.

On the subway platform, while we were waiting for the express train downtown, Mom kept telling everyone to stand back from the tracks, and Dad suddenly said, "Shhh," because the air filled with beautiful music. A Chinese man was playing the violin, and Dad said, "He's a virtuoso!" which means really talented. And we were getting to hear him for free! Or almost—Mom gave Matt a dollar to put in the man's open violin case.

Our subway arrived, and we got into the very first car. Mom sat down on the orange plastic seat, Dad and Uncle Angel stood and held the skinny silver poles, and other subway riders were reading books and Bibles and newspapers. Matt said, "Miguel, follow me!" So Miguel did. Me too. We went to the front window and watched the subway beams light up the dark, lonely tunnel tracks and listened to the roar as we shot through the earth beneath Manhattan.

Miguel **LOVED** it! *"No me lo creo"* (No May Low Cray Oh), he said. "I don't believe it. We are racing under skyscrapers! In a tunnel."

"Fifty miles an hour," Dad called out. "The subways opened over a hundred years ago and they run twenty-four hours a day."

"All the day?" Uncle Angel asked.

"All day long," Dad confirmed.

When I was planning out Miguel's visit, it didn't even occur to me to write down "subway" or "tunnel"—or *túnel* (2 Nell). I wished I were a better tour guide. For a second I almost felt like a tagalong with my family, the way I've been feeling with Cecily and Suze.

The subway got shmooshier and shmooshier because every time a voice said, "Stand clear of the closing doors," more and more people got in. Finally, on Canal Street, we got out, walked up the stairs—and emerged in a whole nother world! (Is "nother" a word?)

CHINATOWN! Signs are in Chinese; phone booths are pagodas; almost everyone is Asian; and street stalls sell everything from live baby turtles, paper lanterns, and tree bark to weird herbs and colorful slippers. Chinatown is as different from Times Square as Times Square is from my neighborhood!

The markets had bundles of dark leafy greens and vegetables that didn't even look familiar. The fish stores sold silver minnows, shiny big-eyed fish, squirming crabs, crawling lobsters, and sea creatures I couldn't name. I held my nose, but Uncle Angel and Miguel recognized the fish and shellfish because most of Spain borders the sea, so Spaniards eat a lot of seafood.

We walked past restaurants with dead ducks hanging from hooks in the window. Ugh! But we were starving, so when Dad said, "How about this one?" Miguel held the door open for everyone and in we went.

Some things on the menu sounded disgusting, like pig knuckles and jellyfish. But we ordered yummy normal things like spare ribs and dumplings. And pork buns! We ordered too much—but ate it all up anyway! We were B.P.s or Big Pigs!

Uncle Angel said that in Valencia, you have to work hard to get a waiter's attention, but that in New York, some waiters keep asking, "Is everything okay?" until you want to say, "Leave us in peace!" (Mom translated.)

After dinner, we went north up Mulberry Street to a café in Little Italy. White Christmasy lights draped from one side of the street to the other in glittery mini canopies.

We sat at an outside table on a narrow street and had pastries called cannoli. Uncle Angel also had a *cigarillo* (C Gar E Yo) and was blowing smoke in gross little rings. He said, "Broadway, China, Italy: *Tres continentes en un día*" (Trace Cone T Nen Tace N

Oon D Ah). Miguel translated: "Three continents in one day!"

Mom said, "I've never thought of it like that."

Matt said, "You should tell him not to smoke."

Mom whispered, "Adults don't tell other adults what to do. Besides, we're outside."

Matt said, "But it's bad for him."

Mom whispered, "You're right, but it's his choice."

Matt said, "Can't he change his choice?"

I said, "Can't *you* change the subject?"

"Okay okay," Matt said. "Who wants to go to the bat room with me?"

Miguel laughed and said, "I." He thinks my family is funny even when I think they're weird.

I guess Miguel really has become a friend of the family, the whole family.

For better and worse!

A few minutes later we were all double-kissing and saying goodbye. New York may be the city that never sleeps, but tourists and natives need shut-eye!

Falling asleeeeeeep — mmmm ...

June 21
4 P.M.

Dear Diary,

To celebrate the first day of summer, Dad took today off, and he and Mom took Miguel, Matt, and me to Jones Beach or *Playa* (Ply Ah). Uncle Angel had to work.

Jones Beach is beautiful! It's about an hour and a half away by car and has perfect waves for boogie boarding. At first, I told Mom I didn't want to go because I might feel self-conscious in a bathing suit. But she reminded me that I love the beach and said I look cute in my bathing suit and should appreciate my body for what it *does* not how it *looks*, and besides, the beach was *full* of bodies, not just mine. I told her she was being teacher-y and added, "I still might wear a shirt on top."

But I didn't. Just sunscreen!

I will say this:

Miguel looks cute
in his swimsuit!

And Mom's right: I love the beach. Especially boogie

boarding. I love catching waves and holding on tight as they take me to shore. And I love grabbing my board and running back in and catching another wave and riding that one to shore too. It's like flying.

In the ocean, nothing stays the same. New waves come crashing in, morning and night, here and in Spain. And you can't plan everything out. You also can't worry about boys or friends or crushes or enemies or *anything*. You have to just pay attention to where the water takes you. And go with the flow. Go for the ride!

Well, Miguel and Matt and I were having fun, but then Matt got cold and asked Miguel to get out with him. I had a lot of sand in my bathing suit (!) and wanted to fix that in the water, so I said, "Go ahead, I'm taking one last ride."

But here's what happened. I caught one last wave, and just when I was about to hop out, I heard a familiar grown-up voice in front of me.

"Melanie Martin? Melanie Martin!"

I looked up from where I'd landed and saw two feet, two ankles, two shins, two knees, two thighs, one pink bikini, and one head that I couldn't make out because the sun was too bright. I started getting up and realized that next to me, wearing nothing but a drippy bathing suit, was . . . Principal Gemunder!

Trust me, nothing is more embarrassing than bumping into your principal in a bikini! And I almost bumped into her *literally*!!

"What a nice surprise!" Principal Gemunder said.

I jumped up so we'd be face to face and I wouldn't accidentally find out whether her belly button was an innie, an outie, or an in-betweenie!

"Hi," I mumbled. I was *not* at my conversational best.

Matt saw us, but he stayed right where he was on the sand. I could tell that he was trying to look sorry for me—but also trying not to laugh.

"Do you have summer plans, Melanie? A camp or a trip?"

"We're not sure, but right now a friend from Spain is here, so we're mostly doing New Yorky things."

No sooner had I said New Yorky
than I knew it sanded dorky.

"How splendid! What part of Spain is she from?"

"Valencia," I mumbled. "He."

Ms. Gemunder's eyebrows went straight up, but she got them to go down again. We weren't at school, so it would have been inappropriate for her to call Miguel's visit inappropriate.

"I hope you have a wonderful time!" she said.

After we said goodbye, I felt stupid and realized I should have asked about *her* summer plans, but I swear, I'd never thought of her as a person with summer plans.

Maybe I thought principals went into a frozen state at their desks all summer, then got thawed out on the first morning of the next school year.

Crazy, right? I mean, my mom's a teacher and I know she has a life. She loves snow days and summertime as much as Matt and I do. But still. I'd just never pictured Ms. Gemunder, my mom's boss, at the beach in a bikini!

Thank God she didn't have a tattoo or anything. I don't think I could have handled that.

Your traumatized
        Friend, Melanie

P.S. Matt understood how dumb I felt at the beach, but I don't think Miguel quite quite quite got it.

Dear Diary,

This is going to sound strange, but it's almost as if Mom, Dad, Miguel, and I just came back from a double date, a date that ended in a weird way.

Mom and Dad had reserved seats to listen to music with grown-up friends, but the friends had to cancel at the last minute, so Mom and Dad decided Miguel and I were old enough to go instead. Not Matt, though. Baby Matt had to stay home with the babysitter. And not Uncle Angel because he had a business dinner.

Mom asked Uncle Angel if it would be okay if Miguel slept over in Matt's room tonight(!) so we wouldn't have to take him back to the hotel. Uncle Angel said *sí*.

Personally, I think Mom and Dad liked being with us as much as they would have liked being with their boring regular friends. I know they like showing Miguel around.

In the car, Dad said, "When people say 'New York City,' they don't mean just Manhattan, they mean all five boroughs."

"Boroughs? *¿Burros?*" (Boo Rrrohs). Miguel looked at Mom. "Donkeys? Asses?"

175

Dad laughed, but Mom said, "In English, a *burro* is a donkey—or ass—but in New York, a 'borough' is a neighborhood or area."

If Matt had been in the backseat, he would have been peeing in his pants.

New York City's five boroughs are:

1. Manhattan (the island where we live)
2. Brooklyn (where we went tonight)
3. Queens (where Miguel and Uncle Angel landed)
4. Staten Island (where you go by ferry)
5. The Bronx (home of the Bronx Zoo and Yankee Stadium)

Dad said, "Tonight we will see the best of Brooklyn." And I think we did!

It's amazing how much of New York I've seen since Monday. And it's only Thursday!

When a family has a guest, they have dinner conversations and don't fight. When a family has out-of-town guests, they get to be tourists in their own hometown.

I can't believe I'd never walked across the Brooklyn Bridge! It's been around since 1883, and I've been around eleven years, and tonight was the first time I ever walked across it.

It's enormous! It has stones and arches like a cathedral, and it attaches Brooklyn to Manhattan, and cars drive over it. Above the cars are paths for walking or biking and benches for sitting.

It was half scary, half exciting.

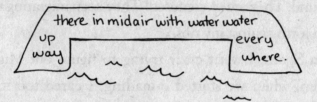

there in midair with water water
up way
every where.

Our feet were safe on the wooden walkway, but it was as if we were tightrope walking. The East River was below us, and all around was air and steel cables. It was so cool I hated to blink! It felt as if we were in the middle of the sky!

Dad said, "When the Brooklyn Bridge was built, people were afraid to cross it, so a famous circus master, P. T. Barnum, led twenty-one elephants across to prove it wasn't dangerous."

Miguel laughed, and Mom took a picture of him and me with the lacy white Woolworth Building sticking up behind us. It used to be the tallest building in the world—until the Chrysler Building came along, and many others after that.

I said, "It's beautiful."

Miguel turned right to me and repeated, "Beautiful."

I looked at him and wasn't sure if he was complimenting the skyline—or me. Well, after that I couldn't say anything! But my stomach butterflies started flapping around. They are so confused! They keep migrating back and forth against my ribs.

In Spain, I went crazy trying to figure out Miguel. Then, when we started e-mailing, I cared too much about whether he wrote back. Which may be normal for first love or whatever, but it was a lot of anxiety for a worrier like me. So now I'm trying to figure out how to care about someone without losing my mind.

I mean, I need my mind. I don't like when it's lost.

Anyway, we had pizza for dinner at a restaurant right under the bridge called Grimaldi's. It had red-and-white-checked tablecloths. Miguel cut his pizza into pieces and ate with a fork and knife! That's what they do in Spain. So I did too. Mom looked surprised, but she smiled and didn't say anything.

For dessert, we ate chocolate chip ice cream cones outside at the Fulton Ferry Landing. Bright yellow water taxis docked at a fancy restaurant called River Café. Miguel said, "I have never seen a taxi boat." I hadn't either, but I didn't want to admit that.

A big red sign flashed 77 degrees Fahrenheit (which made sense to us), then 25 degrees Celsius (which made sense to Miguel).

Mom looked out toward the lights of Manhattan and said, "Feel the summer breeze. The *brisa*" (Bree Sa).

Dad put his arms around her, and for a second, I wondered whether Miguel would put his arms around me. He gave me a shy smile and I smiled back. But no touching.

We read part of a poem stenciled into the railing. It's by Walt Whitman, who lived in Brooklyn. One line is: "throw out questions and answers!"

At first I thought Whitman meant "throw out" like throw away, discard, delete, or get rid of. (Not to sound like a thesaurus.)

Now I think he probably meant: Keep coming up with questions and answers. Keep asking and answering! Keep thinking!

Here's the thing: Sometimes I can't *stop* thinking. I've even been asking myself things like: How different are friendship and love? If that were a math question, would friendship and love be separate spots on the same line, or would they be intersecting circles? What about obsession?

At 7:30, the Bargemusic concert started, so we went into a big room that actually floats right *on* the water. *On* the East River! The room rocked a teeny bit! It had big picture windows, and we looked out at Manhattan and saw boats and birds gliding by and saw the sky s-l-o-w-l-y change from pinkish blue to deep blue to black. The buildings changed color too. They went from beige gray to sunset gold to black (actually, black with twinkling office lights).

Mostly we watched the two pianists.

Miguel and I sat in the front row. We could see their hands as they touched and pressed and stroked and pounded and banged and caressed the keys. It was not the kind of music I usually listen to, but it was pretty and romantic and boring only in parts.

It's cool how different musicians get such different sounds out of the same notes. And different writers get such different books out of the same letters. And different artists (Mom would add) get such different paintings out of the same colors.

Well, the two pianos were facing each other. They weren't baby grand pianos or regular upright pianos or dinky electric pianos but great big jumbo grand pianos. The stretch limos of pianodom.

There was a man pianist and a woman pianist. (When Matt says "pianist," it sounds like a totally different word, which I'm not going to write but which, I will say, only one of those two pianists has.)

Anyway, the two pianists started out far away across from each other on the separate pianos.

Later they sat down again, but together on the *same* bench so that they could play side by side.

I liked how they were far away, then got closer. Is that what Miguel and I are doing—getting closer?

Miguel leaned over and whispered, "May Lah Nee, I will never forget this night."

I whispered, "Me neither."

I dangled my fingers next to his chair,
but all they touched was air air air.

191

The final piece was a two-piano version of George Gershwin's *Rhapsody* in Blue*. At the end, everybody clapped loudly—except one man who blew his nose honkingly.

The melody got stuck in my head and I didn't even mind, which I usually do. On the drive home, we all hummed it—for about a *minuto* (Me New Toe). Dad said George Gershwin died young, but first he and his brother, Ira, and another guy wrote a Great American Opera: *Porgy and Bess*. Mom started singing "Summertime, and the living is eeeeasyyyy," and Miguel smiled at me because he's getting used to Mom's singing—and my getting embarrassed.

When we got home, Mom and Dad said good night, and Miguel and I hesitated in the hallway. I was on my way to my room and he was on his way to Matt's room, where Matt was already asleep.

Suddenly Miguel gave me Spanish double cheek kisses and cupped his hand around my upper arm. His fingertips felt warm, and he pressed very gently. I took a baby step toward him. The evening had felt romantic (duh! no Matt the Brat!) and we were looking at each other without saying anything, and I thought *un besito* might feel really nice. I even thought the moment was right.

But instead of puckering up and maybe half-closing my eyes, I chickened out and accidentally broke the mood. I talked! "So are you having fun in New York?"

"New York is a marvel," he said. "And your parents are very good to me." Then he said *"Buenas noches,"* and taught me how to say "Sweet dreams" in Spanish. It's *Sueña con los ángeles* (Sway Nya Cone Lohs On Hell Ays), which does not mean "Dream of Los Angeles." It means "Dream with the angels."

I said it back to him. But his eyes looked a little serious. Or sad. Or as if something might be bothering him.

What do you think?

Throwing out questions, ?

? New York Me!

*Diary entries aren't supposed to have footnotes, but I had to look up "rhapsody" because I had noooo idea how to spell it. My dictionary says it's an "extravagantly enthusiastic expression of feeling." Sometimes I feel extravagantly enthusiastic and expressive, but right now, I'm more pensive than rhapsodic. I'm also sleepy. Is Miguel? I hope the mice on the Ferris wheel don't keep him up. Matt's room can be pretty noisy at night. Then again, maybe he is already asleep.**

** Asleep is what I soon will be —
That's it for now from Melanie!

6/22 Friday morning ☀

Dear Diary,

This morning was seriously embarrassing!!! I know I get embarrassed easily, but I could send what happened today into a magazine! Not that I would! That would be even MORE embarrassing!

It was about eight. I heard Matt and Miguel talking, so I figured I might as well get up too.

The *problema* (Pro Blame Ah) was that when I wake

up, I never stay in bed trying to remember my dreams or plan my day or think my thoughts; I head straight to the bathroom.

Well, I didn't want to stagger down the hall in my pajamas with Miguel in Matt's room, but I also didn't want to have to get all the way dressed, especially since I was going to have to undress to shower.

To make matters worse, my hair was spiky. I looked as if I were entering a Statue of Liberty look-alike contest. I needed to pat the spikes down with water—but I needed to get to the bathroom to get to the water.

Who knew it would be soooo complicated to have Miguel sleep over? It made me glad he slept at the hotel the first nights!

I thought about putting on lip gloss, but that seemed like a dumb thing to do before brushing my teeth. So I decided to make a run for it. Five, four, three, two, one. I figured I probably wouldn't bump into Miguel and how bad would it be if I did?

Answer: VERY BAD!!!

Right when I was about to walk *into* the bathroom, who should walk *out* of the bathroom? Miguel! Looking great! He was all showered and dressed and his hair was combed and he looked very handsome or *muy guapo* (Mooey Gwa Po).

I couldn't exactly shove past him or pretend I didn't recognize him! So I mumbled *hola* and he mumbled hi and we both smiled and that's when I realized I still had my retainer in my mouth. I *never* wear it in public! But I *never* think of my hallway as public!

It was so mortifying I shut myself in the bathroom and ran the tap water while I peed. (I didn't want anyone hearing!!) Then I took a ridiculously long shower because I was not ready to face Miguel again.

Finally I knew that if I didn't come out, I would shrivel up. My fingertips were wreally wreally wreally wrinkly, and it was definitely time to get out. So I did. And I was all set to towel off when I realized something terrible: There was no towel.

No towel!!!

I said, "Mom! I need a towel," but she didn't hear me. I knew Dad had gone to work, so I called out, "Mom! Matt! Towel!!" but again, nothing. Then I shouted, "TOWEL!!!" fairly loudly, sure that this time Matt might tease me or even try to charge money but at least come to my rescue with a stupid towel.

No such luck.

I assumed they had the TV on and couldn't hear me, so finally I yelled at the top of my lungs:

"TOWEL!!!"

Miguel's voice gently asked, "May Lah Nee, is something wrong?"

I said, "Is my mom nearby?"

"She went to the corner to buy eggs."

"And Matt?"

"He has accompanied her."

"Oh," I said from my side of the bathroom door, sopping wet and stark raving naked (if you don't count my necklace). I could either stand there and drip-dry, which would take a while, or ask Miguel for a towel. Two terrible options.

I remembered that in Spanish, "towel" is *toalla*, so that's what I said, but really softly.

"Could you hand me a Toe Eye Ah please?"

Believe it or not, I could hear Miguel laugh a little. Not a cracking-up Matt the Brat laugh. And not an Oozy Soozy hyena laugh. Just a sweet amused laugh.

"Where are the towels, May Lah Nee?"

"In the closet in the hallway. Behind you."

I heard footsteps, a door open and shut, and more footsteps. "I hold it for you?"

"*Sí*," I said, and stuck my damp arm out the bathroom door. He handed over the towel, and I took it and shut the door and dried off and tried very hard not to die of embarrassment.

Has anyone ever died of embarrassment? Probably not because if so, I wouldn't be writing in you, I'd be resting in peace! R.I.P.

I dried off and brushed my teeth and was about to gargle. But I didn't want Miguel to hear me go Swish Swish Gurgle Gurgle Splat, so I decided not to.

I hadn't brought any clothes to the bathroom, and I didn't want to come out wrapped in just the Toe Eye Ah. So I got back in my pajamas and prayed I wouldn't run into Miguel again until I was fully dressed.

And I didn't.

He probably stayed out of the way on purpose to be polite. Me, I've been hiding in my bedroom writing in you. I know I need to go have breakfast, but this day has already been traumatic and it's not even nine.

YOURS IN HIDING,
morningtime Mel

Dear Diary,   Same day, about to leave ———▷

"*¡Riquíssimo!*" (Rrree Key See Mo) That's what Miguel said about Mom's chocolate chip pancakes and blueberry pancakes. Delicious! He'd never tried either kind before.

Afterward, though, while we were doing the breakfast dishes, he was being very quiet. The way he'd been in the hallway last night. I was really really really tempted to ask, "What are you thinking?"

I wasn't sure if he'd say, "About you—I had missed you, May Lah Nee!" Or "May Lah Nee, I *would* like to kiss you!" Or, God forbid, "I must tell you, May Lah Nee, about a girl in my math class . . ."

One way to find out.

But I wasn't quite brave enough. So I decided to say something easier. Something about the necklace he gave me that was now back on my neck.

I said, *"Plátano. Bonito."*

He said, "Pretty banana?"

"Banana?!"

"¿Plátano?"

"I meant silver."

"¡Plata!" He laughed, so I did too.

"I just wanted to say that my necklace is pretty."

"It is pretty on you, May Lah Nee."

I smiled and asked, "Miguel, are you homesick?"

"Sick?" he repeated. I explained the question, and he answered, "No. I am not homesick. I like being with your family."

I figured now or never. "What were you thinking before? When you were being so quiet?"

Miguel took a breath and met my eyes. "I am not homesick, but I was thinking about my home. I am hoping my parents can to get along with each other as I get along with them. While I am here, they are taking a trip and trying to resolve problems. You know this?"

"Yes." What I didn't add was that I'd completely forgotten about it.

"They argued and had many discussions this spring. It was difficult for them. And for me." I handed Miguel Matt's breakfast plate. I knew it was Matt's because Matt had smeared his leftover melty chocolate chips into two blobs and a curve. Miguel looked at the smiley on the plate, dunked it into warm water, then handed it back to me, blank. "I am sorry I didn't write to you many e-mails during that time."

"No, Miguel, *I* am sorry." And I was. Sorry he was sad. And sorry that I'd been so concerned about me and my feelings that I hadn't thought about him and his feelings. I mean, poor Miguel! The whole time I was worrying about whether he liked me, he was worrying about whether his parents could still like each other. "I hope things work out," I said.

"Work out? Exercise?"

"No. Get better. Get fixed up."

"Oh yes, work out." Our eyes met. "Thank you, May Lah Nee."

191

Matt raced into the kitchen and said, "Miguel, do you like dinosaurs?"

Miguel winked at me. "I have never met a dinosaur."

Mom joined us. "Well, it's high time. But before we set off, Miguel, why don't you send a quick e-mail to your parents?"

While he's writing to them, I'm writing in you.

Tonight, after the dinos, Dad and Uncle Angel will meet us for a picnic on the Great Lawn in Central Park to hear a free opera. ($ince opera i$ $o expen$ive, Dad love$ when it'$ free.)

The opera is called *The Elixir of Love*, which means "Love Potion." Sounds embarrassing, but it doesn't matter since it's in Italian. Dad said it's about a girl, Adina, who didn't know she loved a guy, Nemorino, then realizes she does. I asked, "What about the Love Potion?"

Dad smiled. "Wine."

"Love" in Italian is *amore* (Ah More Ay). In Spanish, it's *amor* (Ah More). Is that how love might sometimes feel? Ah, More! Ah!! More!! Ahhh!!! More!!!

Love,
May Lah Lah Lah Nee

Dear Diary,

Ever since Miguel arrived, I've been hoping to have some time alone with him, just us. (The towel emergency does not count!) Today Mom helped that happen.

We entered the American Museum of Natural History through the door next to the statue of Theodore Roosevelt. Matt said, "Tell Miguel about teddy bears."

I said, "You tell."

Matt began, "You know DogDog and Hedgehog?"

"Why would Miguel know about our stuffed animals?" I practically hissed. "Besides, they have nothing to do with this story."

Matt shrugged. "President Teddy Roosevelt liked to hunt, and once, in Mississippi"—Matt looked at Mom and she nodded—"he went hunting, and there was a bear cub that he could have killed but decided not to. He *spared* it. Well, newspapers ran cartoons about it, and a toymaker began making soft little bears and calling them teddy bears because of Teddy Roosevelt. Soon every kid wanted a little bear."

"*Osito*" (Oh Sea Toe), I said, since I knew that word.

"I don't mean *every* single kid wanted a teddy," Matt went on. "I have a dog—DogDog—and Melanie has"—he looked at me, I glared, he stopped midsentence, and Miguel looked amused. Then

We walked through the doors and saw... dinosaurs!!!

One is an unbelievably tall *Barosaurus* with an unbelievably dinky head.

"*Dinosaurio*" (D No Sour E O), I said.

Mom gave us paper bracelets to put on (at the Met, they give you metal buttons), and Matt said, "Let's go see the thirty-four-ton meteor!"

Mom said, "I don't think Miguel should miss the other dinosaurs. You do want to see them, don't you, Miguel?"

Miguel said, "If it is possible."

"*Posible*" (Poe See Blay), I said, because I was on a roll with my one-word translations.

"Tell you what," Mom said, "Melanie and Miguel will do the dinos, and Matt and I will see the meteors and—"

"Shrunken heads!!" Matt said. "And naked cave people!!"

"Whatever. Then we'll meet under the whale in exactly one hour. Okay?"

"Okay," I said, though I was shocked. I'm always b-e-g-g-i-n-g Mom to let me go places without her, and she always says no. When I say, "Why not?" she says she trusts *me* but not the world.

I must have looked funny because Mom said, "Unless you'd rather we all stick together?"

"No!!"

"You two will be fine inside here," Mom said. "Just take care of each other."

That sounded embarrassing, but it was worse when she added, "Don't look like you've never been on your own before. Look confident. And if someone approaches you, walk away or—"

"I know, I know, find a guard," I said.

"Right." Ever since I was born, Mom has been lecturing me about how if someone creepy says, "Would you like some candy?" or "Can you help me find my lost puppy?" I should run away or scream or find a police officer or mom or doorman or Safe Haven. Not that this has ever happened.

People think New York City is more dangerous than it actually is.

"We'll be fine, Me Ron Dah," Miguel told Mom. "We will meet you at twelve minus fifteen."

"Eleven forty-five," Mom said. "That's how we say it. Or a quarter to twelve."

"A quarter to twelve," Miguel repeated. Then we took off—alone! At first I kept turning around to look for Mom because it was hard to believe we were really on our own.

Next thing you know, Miguel and I were staring at the enormous, bony, sixty-five-million-year-old head of a *Tyrannosaurus rex*. The caption said it got dug up in Montana in 1908, but all I could think of to say was that it was big big big. So I said, *"Grande grande grande"* (Gron Day Gron Day Gron Day).

Nearby was a giant put-together skeleton of a carnosaur. The caption said it was probably aggressive and ferocious, but all I could think to add was that it was old old old. So I said, *"Viejo viejo viejo"* (Byay Hhho Byay Hhho Byay Hhho).

It was weird. There I was with triceratopses and

stegosauri and woolly mammoths and Miguel all to myself, and I couldn't think of *anything* worthwhile to say.

I almost started wishing Little Science Boy were there to babble about Jurassic ecosystems.

We passed a nest with dino eggs. "*Huevos*" (Way Vohs), I said.

He said, "It's hard to believe that birds and dinosaurs are cousins, true?"

"True. Miguel, in Spain, do you have the old TV show *Friends*?"

"*Amigos* (Ah Me Goes). *Sí.*"

"This is where Ross works! He's a paleontologist."

"Really?"

"Yes. And I wish I were because I'd be a better tour guide. All I know about dinosaurs is that they're *grande*, *viejo*, and extinct-o."

"*Extinto*" (S Teen Toe), Miguel corrected. "May Lah Nee, I do not expect you to be a tour guide or *paleontóloga* (Pa Lay Own Toe Low Ga). I came so my parents could have time alone, *sí*, but I also came to be with your parents. And Matt. And you."

He smiled and I smiled back and our eyes locked and suddenly I couldn't have looked away even if I'd wanted to. Which I didn't. It was as if we finally *were* all alone in the museum, in New York, in America, in the world! It was like a Perfect Moment or Mo-

mento Perfecto (Mo Men Toe Pair Fec Toe). Miguel stepped a little closer, and for a second, I was pretty positive that he was reaching for my hand. And that I wanted him to. It was practically making me dizzzzzy.

Then, out of the corner of my eye (or maybe the angle, since eyes don't have corners), I saw someone bounding up to us. At first I thought it was Matt the Brat. But it was . . . Suze the Ooze! With her older sister.

I wanted to hide Miguel behind the duck-billed hadrosaur, but it was too late (and dino skeletons are see-through anyway).

"Melanie!! Hi!!"

Suze was staring at Miguel, so I had no choice but to introduce them. Miguel gave her little cheek kisses, which (I now of course know) everyone does in Spain. But it was soooo frustrating because seconds earlier it had seemed like he and I were finally going to hold hands—and now he was kissing Suze!! Suze!!!

"I am Miguel," he said, and instead of saying, "I am Susan" or "I am Suze" or even "I am a horrible person with horrible timing who specializes in ruining everything for everybody," she turned to me, her eyes popping out, and said, "Omigod!! Your Spanish boyfriend!!"

Omigod, I wanted to die! But I wanted to kill her first!! I did *not* want Miguel to think that I go around calling him my boyfriend, especially since I don't.

I also didn't want him to think that I hated the idea!

She lowered her voice and added, "No offense, but I pictured him older."

Now I really wanted to punch her little face in! I wished Miguel and I had gone with Mom and Matt to the disgusting shrunken-head exhibit. No! I wished I could have shrunken *Suze's* head!

I somehow managed to say, "Miguel is my *amigo*. And he speaks English!"

"Oh!!" Suze turned to him and started talking loudly and slowly as if there were something wrong with his ears. "IS MELANIE SHOWING YOU AROUND?"

This was torture!

"Yes," he said. He gave me a little smile.

"HOW LONG ARE YOU HERE?"

"Three more days."

I wanted to say, "He's Spanish, not hard of hearing," but I just stood there.

"DO YOU LIKE NEW YORK?"

"It is stupendous," Miguel said, probably because *estupendo* (S 2 Pen Dough) is a normal Spanish word.

This was worse than a dentist appointment! Finally I announced, "Well, we have to go."

"Wait, Mel," Suze said. "My mom's letting me have a pizza party tomorrow. A lot of people are coming. Justin said he'd be there, but Cecily is away."

"I know," I said. "With her dad."

"Want to come?"

"That is a nice invitation," Miguel said, just when I was trying to figure out how to say, "In your dreams!" I couldn't believe Suze. In no time, I'd gone from Perfect Moment to Stinky Moment. Plus, when she mentioned Justin, part of my brain started thinking about him, which was distracting—and not what I needed.

"My parents may have plans for us," I informed Suze. "I'll call you, okay?"

"Okay."

In the elevator, Miguel said, "A party—I could meet your friends."

"Maybe," I said, "but my best *amiga* isn't here this week. . . ." I didn't add, "And besides, it's easier to have you all to myself."

Truth is, I would have liked for Miguel to meet Cecily. But I couldn't picture him meeting Justin. ("Miguel, meet Justin. I sorta like him too!")

On the long walk to the Hall of Ocean Life, I told Miguel that Suze is not my favorite *persona* (Pair Sohn Ah). I even told him about her dumb habit of always saying "No offense" right before saying something offensive.

Matt saw us and came running over. "Isn't it cool?!?"

Miguel said, "What?"

Matt said, "Moby Dick!!" He pointed at the life-size whale hanging down from the ceiling.

Miguel said, "He's bigger than the dinosaurs!"

"Blue whales can be almost as long as three school buses," Matt said. "This one is ninety-four feet and has a belly button!"

"He is stupendous!" Miguel said.

Matt laughed. "No one says 'stupendous'!"

202

"No?" He looked at me. "Then he is phenomenal!"

"That's even worse. Just say 'awesome.'" Matt smiled. "Or 'cool.'"

"Cool!" Miguel said, and I wished I had been comfortable enough to tell him that.

Mom said, "When Melanie and Matt were little, we *lived* here, especially in the winter! The kids loved this place—the gems and minerals and running under the whale—"

"Mom!" With my eyes, I begged her to quit reminiscing about my Pigtail Childhood. Fortunately she changed the subject. "I got tickets to a show at the planetarium. It's called 'Passport to the Universe.'"

"Did you bring our passports?" Matt asked, but Mom said we wouldn't need them.

We walked to the planetarium, and instead of thinking about long-ago dinosaurs or far-off galaxies, I was thinking about Suze and how mad I was at her for interrupting Miguel and me and getting me thinking about Justin, who had nothing to do with anything and should not have been taking up any of my brain molecules right then.

Too late. My brain was off and running. Miguel and Justin are both my *amigos*. One lives far away and one lives nearby, and thinking about either one of them can get me good nervous (excited) or bad nervous (upset). They're both smart and cute and nice. Miguel is gallant and gave me a necklace and my whole family likes him. Justin is funny and lives nearby and I usually feel comfortable with him. I like e-mailing them both, and I like when they explain things to me, whether about Spain or math or anything.

So what am I supposed to do about stupid Suze's stupid party??

Mom led us to a waiting area, where TV monitors explained light-years and said it takes eight minutes for a sun ray to reach Earth.

Matt said, "What are a Martian's favorite candies?"

Miguel said, "I do not know."

"Milky Ways and Mars Bars! I made that up!" Mom had to translate.

Tom Hanks's voice came on the monitor. A camera zoomed in on people rushing around, then pulled back back back until it showed the street, the neighborhood, the city, the Earth, the planets, and a gazillion stars!

Tom Hanks announced, "There comes a time in each of our lives when it dawns on us that we are *not* the center of the universe."

Well, that got me thinking. Have I reached that time in *my* life yet? I can tell you, since you're my diary, that I know I *should* worry about war and homelessness and global warming and terrorism and other people's parents, and I do (a little), but I also have to admit (just to you) that I worry more about Miguel and Justin and Cecily and Suze and Matt the Brat and my mice and my parents and myself.

We finally entered the planetarium. The room was dark and the ceiling was round and a light made Matt's shoelaces purple.

We sat down and it got pitch-black, and I realized how tired I was from waking up early, staying up late, walking walking walking, and trying to figure out boys and friends and whether I was just an itsy-bitsy teeny tiny speck in the vast, gigantic observable universe.

Miguel sat next to me, and I could just have reached

over and held his hand. Thirty minutes ago, we *had* almost held hands. Now that feeling seemed as far away as the Milky Way. How come the connection between us sometimes feels so strong and sometimes feels so fragile?

I leaned further back in my comfortable seat, and a million billion trillion stars appeared above us, and soft calming music surrounded us, and Tom Hanks droned on about the golden age of astronomy and how we are all citizens of the cosmos.

It was humbling. And overwhelming.

I closed my eyes for a split second, and then, somehow, I . . . fell asleep! I slept through the entire show! My brain was on overload and must have just shut down and crashed, like a computer.

When the lights went back on, Mom nudged me and said we should go home and get some rest before the opera.

So we went outside, and I stuck my hand up—which I've been doing since I was a little kid. (Mom says "taxi" was one of my first words.)

Miguel said, "There's one!"

I said, "No, it's got someone in it."

He looked at me. "How do you know?"

I explained that when a cab is available, its top light is on. Lots of yellow cabs streamed by us, but their top lights were off, meaning the taxis were full. Some had two little top lights on, but that meant that the drivers or *taxistas* (Ta Sees Stahs) were off duty.

"Should I get a gypsy?" I asked. Mom nodded, so I flagged one and it pulled over.

Miguel said, "This car is not yellow and it has no light. How did you know it was a taxi?"

I explained that I'd spotted the sign in the passenger-seat windshield and had noticed just one person in the car.

"Oh," Miguel said.

"We call them gypsy cabs," I added.

"Gypsy?" Miguel asked, and next thing you know, he and Mom were talking about a Spanish writer named García Lorca, who wrote poems about gypsies, the moon, and even New York. Mom said Lorca also wrote a tragic play called *The House of Bernarda Alba*.

Well, as we got closer and closer to *The Apartment*

of Melanie Martin, I started thinking about all the differences between Miguel and me. Different ages and languages and countries and cultures and experiences. Miguel was squooshed next to me, but I don't know if he even noticed because he and Mom were talking a mile a minute in Spanish. Is that how she'd babbled to Miguel's father, Antonio? She switched to English to tell me that Lorca got murdered in the Spanish Civil War. I said, "That's terrible," but until that minute I'd never heard of Lorca, so it's not as if I was sad sad sad.

More like: I felt *estúpida* (S 2 Pee Da) for not caring about the Great Spanish Poet.

While they talked, I also felt a little left out. But I reminded myself that if Miguel and I are really *amigos*, I should be hoping things get better between his parents, not just that they get "better" between us. I should care about him, not just how much he cares about me.

I was also thinking that it's hard to care about two boys at the same time, especially when they are from different worlds.

We got to our apartment, the cab stopped, and

Miguel started to open his door on the traffic side—not the building side. New Yorkers know *never* to do that. The driver shouted, "Close the door!" and Mom gave Miguel the little lecture she used to have to give us.

At home, Mom sliced up a cantaloupe, and Matt said it tasted melony, and Miguel repeated, "May Lah Nee?" and everyone laughed. Then he told Mom about Suze's *invitación* (Een B Ta Syone), and Mom said that sounded fun. Fun?!

Miguel and Mom are now at Zabar's buying cheese, salami, bread, pasta, fruit, and brownies for our picnic at tonight's opera. I stayed here. Guess what I have been doing? Hint: Scribble, scribble, scribble.

I also cleaned my room. First I hid Hedgehog in my sock drawer, but then I felt guilty and sorry for her, so I pulled her out and put her right back on my bed where she belongs.

Your amiga,

Melony Martin,
CItIzen of the Cosmos,
• Dot in the Universe

one *hora* (Or Ah) or hour later

Dear Diary,

Miguel just came into my room and saw the heart-shaped frame with the photo of us at the castle. I should have hidden *that* in my sock drawer! I was soooo embarrassed, as he could tell. He said, "May Lah Nee, I have a very nice photo of you on my—how do you say?—bullet board."

"Bulletin board?"

"*Sí sí.* Bulletin board."

I confess. That made me feel better!

Photogenically,
May Lah Nee Mar Teen

Friday night at my 👓←desk

Dear Diary,

I have to tell you something.

Things keep changing.

Tonight in Central Park, Miguel tried to put his arm around me.

I'm pretty sure he did anyway.

We were sitting on our blanket behind Mom, Dad, and Uncle Angel, who were totally into the opera. Matt was busy driving his favorite red car around an imaginary racetrack on our blanket. (Pathetic but true.) Miguel was on my left, and he moved closer and stuck his hand out behind me—not actually over my shoulder or anything—but behind me in what I guess my life-skills teacher would call my personal space. Then he lifted his arms up like he was about to yawn, but he didn't yawn, he kind of lowered his right arm on my back and shoulders.

I didn't move. I didn't plunk my arm around him or scrunch closer or rest my head on his shoulder or *anything*. I just sat there frozen and pretended I hadn't noticed.

Which was dumb. Of course I'd noticed! Who wouldn't notice the weight and warmth of a boy's arm on your back? But I swear, I'd turned into a melon. May Lah Nee the *Melón* (May Loan). I'd gone completely still inside and outside. I'd become a thing instead of a person. An *it* instead of a *she*.

Why why why? Was it because I couldn't bring myself

to do anything with my parents right there? I tried sticking my arm up and over Miguel's back. But it wouldn't go. Gravity was holding it down.

I was the opposite of that *Turandot* lady in the other opera. When she got kissed, she melted. But when Miguel tried to put his arm around me, I went into melon mode!

Thing is, when a boy and a girl are dancing, they're supposed to smoosh together. It's expected, so it feels easier.

Well, I finally got myself to lean into Miguel a teeny bit, and I even put my left arm behind his back— though it was not touching his back.

Miguel turned his head and smiled at me, and I smiled back, and then with his hand, he pulled me a little closer to him. Which felt okay . . . but not one hundred percent *perfecto*.

Dad turned and asked if we liked the opera, and Miguel dropped his hand straight down to the blanket, where it stayed for the rest of the opera. (I doubt Dad even saw.)

When Dad looked away again, Miguel put his right hand on top of my left hand. And it was nice-ish, at first, but then (is this dorky?) I wanted to eat another brownie, and I worried it would seem unfriendly to pull my hand away. So I let it stay there, trapped.

Is there something wrong with me? Is it normal to think like this?

Probably. A lot of weird stuff is normal. But still, you'd think I would have wanted his hand to be covering mine. Hearts really are hard to predict! I guess you can't plan love out. Because sometimes a guy and a girl who like-like each other start just plain liking each other, and sometimes maybe two people who start as friends can become more.

After a while, I said, "Miguel, I have cards."

"Cards?" I pulled out my hand and pulled out my deck, and we taught each other card games while the opera singers serenaded us. We played until the evening twilight became nighttime darkness. Then Mom lit two candles and we played some more. To tell you the truth, I think Miguel liked playing cards. He didn't seem heartbroken or anything. He seemed fine.

I wonder if he's ever thought, as I'm starting to, that if you really care about someone you'll barely ever be able to see, it's mostly going to hurt. I mean, if you love an actor or musician or athlete, you don't sit there hoping for e-mails or IMs or calls or kisses, so it's not hard. But if you love someone you actually know who is far away, you start wanting that person to be closer. You do. And that is not fun. It's also probably the last thing Miguel needs if he's already worried about his parents.

At the end of the opera, Mom and Dad and Uncle Angel were all happy happy happy and Matt was out cold. Uncle Angel said, "It would be nice to leave here."

Mom assured him that we were leaving.

Uncle Angel said, "No, I mean to say, 'to liiiiiive here.'"

Mom laughed. "It *is* nice to live here, but it is also time to leave."

She nudged Matt awake, and we walked with a crowd of other people to the edge of the park. Mom was holding our blanket, Dad was carrying Matt, Uncle Angel was smoking (I could see the fiery glow of his cigarette), and Mom told Miguel and me to get taxis.

"We could get a gypsy," Miguel said.

"*Gitano*" (Hhhe Tah No), I said, and he smiled. I think he likes my little one-word offerings. I also think that somehow Miguel and I will be able to be friends, even if we may not become a mushy couple.

"I see a yellow cab with a light on top!" Miguel said, and put his hand up. The cab screeched to a stop.

Miguel looked proud of himself, so I said, "You're becoming a real New Yorker!"

We all double-kissed in the dark, and Miguel and Uncle Angel got in that cab, and we four M's got in another.

And now here I am, at my desk.

If this were a novel, not a diary, by now Miguel and I might be madly in love and making out every minute—or we might hate each other and be in a big fat fight.

But real life is foggier than fiction.

Really yours,

Mel, who is falling asleep with a pen in her handddd

elevenish

Dear Diary,

What I'm about to write may take you by surprise.

Miguel and Angel are spending a nephew-uncle day downtown, just the two of them (visiting the New York Stock Exchange and riding on the Staten Island Ferry), and I don't feel left out.

I feel sort of relieved. I'm hanging out with Matt in my pajamas, playing with our mice, and it's fine! Is it strange to feel content with my younger brother instead of older boyfriend, or sort-of boyfriend, or ex-boyfriend, or close-but-faraway-regular-friend, or whatever he is?

A few weeks ago, my moods revolved around every e-mail I did or didn't get. I was on a big roller coaster, or as Miguel said they say in Spanish, a Russian mountain or *montaña rusa* (Moan Tahn Ya Rrroo Sa). Now Miguel is here, and you'd think I'd want to be out with him every single second instead of inside with Matt and the mice mice mice.

Maybe it's easier to fall in love than to stay in love. Easier to flirt than to be there for each other 24/7. Easier to think about boys than to hang out with boys. Easier to be a guest than a host. Easier to go crazy about someone who seems to know everything about Spanish and Spain than someone who asks questions about America and English.

Matt must have inherited some of Mom's mind-reading genes because he said, "You know how Miguel sometimes says things funny? Like one time he said, 'The drop that made the cup overflow' instead of 'The straw that broke the camel's back'?"

"I guess . . ."

"Well, he told me that even when people speak a language perfectly, you can usually still tell if they are spies."

"How?"

"You make them do hard math problems, fast and out loud. Most people can't do math except in their own language."

"Oh." But I wasn't thinking about spies. I was thinking about the party tonight with Justin and Miguel.

I wish Miguel hadn't mentioned Suze's party to Mom and Dad. But they probably think it's good for Miguel to be included in a genuine American party. Or maybe they want to have an evening off by themselves too.

OFF and ON
MEL

P.S. Matt showed me his latest crafts project: He's been rolling paper cigarettes. I said, "Mom and Dad would not approve!!"

He said, "I'm not going to *start* smoking, Melanie!! I'm going to help Uncle Angel *stop* smoking."

He showed me how he used black marker to darken the tips of the fake cigarettes. "I'm making him a pack of safe cigarettes."

"It won't work," I said.

"It won't hurt," he replied.

oneish

Dear Diary,

Cecily and I have been IMing. I could have called her, but she's with her dad and, strange but true, lately I've been thinking that sometimes when you IM, you can say more (even though you can also get misunderstood).

Here's the thing: When I'm typing serious stuff, I have to look at my fingers, and that can be hard. But when I'm saying serious stuff in person, I have to look at the other person's eyes, and that can be even harder!

Anyway, when I signed on and saw Cecily's screen name, I wrote: u there?

She wrote: yup

I wrote: how's cheshire your pretty kitty? >^..^< because I love Cheshire and I love making my little cat.

She wrote: fine. At least he was when I left

I typed: i'm confused :-[

She wrote: about chesh?

I wrote: about everything

She wrote: what do u mean?

I wrote: don't tell sooz, k?

She wrote: :-x which means her lips were sealed.

I wrote: promise?

She wrote: mel, suze and i r friends but u and i r bff's

I wrote: awwww because it felt really really really good

to read that I was her best friend forever. Then I just plain typed: i don't know who i like . . . miguel or justin!

I sort of squinted my eyes and stared at the blank screen and was glad I didn't have to watch her reaction. It was taking her a long time to answer, so finally, to be funny, I corrected my grammar and sent: whom

Another five seconds went by, so I added: sry, do u mind if I talk about miguel?

Up popped Cecily's reply to my original confession: do u have 2 choose?

don't i?

i dunno. justin is nice and cute

u don't think miguel is cute?

i haven't met him, remember? he's cute in photos!

in person 2

and u don't have 2 apologize 4 talking about him :-)

:-)

can't u b friends with both and c what happens?

harder than it sounds

i'm trying to help!

i know. i can b friends w/ both but i don't

think i can b more than friends w/ both.

how does justin feel?

i don't know!!! but is it ok if i don't
like miguel in the exact same way i used 2?
it makes me feel sad and guilty just 2 write
that :-(

of course it's ok

what changed?

i dunno.

I didn't want to write: I started thinking about Justin. Or Miguel likes my family and squirrels as much as he likes me. Or he says "stupendous." Or I wanted to kiss him but I couldn't and then he tried to put his arm around me and I turned into a melon. So I wrote:

Miguel is sooo nice! But maybe we're better
as amigos. i'm not ready 2 b so serious w/
someone so far away. Maybe he's not either? Or
maybe Suze is right and i *liked* that he was
far away! Anyway, now that he's here it's
harder 2 b madly in love every single second

mel, u r complicated!

i know. :-(actually my family *is* madly

in love with him! do u think i started liking
miguel just 2 carry on the family tradition?

huh?

the hot romance between my mom and his dad?

wut???

remember those gorilla babies who copied
their parents?

yeah

was i just copying my mom? falling 4 her
bf's son?

i'm not a shrink but if he'd been a weirdo, u wud never
have liked him in the 1st place. trust me!

i trust u. do u think miguel and i were
meant 4 each other? Or made 4 each other??

i don't think anybody is made 4 anybody else. my parents
weren't made 4 each other but i'm glad they made me!

i'm glad 2 :-)

so r u going 2 dump him?

i don't know if we're even going out. r we
going out or hanging out?

he did NOT fly over 2 see the Statue of Liberty. he came
2 see the Beauty of Melanie LOL

hehe but u know what? he also came becz his parents r separated and r trying to work on their marriage

really?? i didn't know that. poor miguel!! :-(

maybe he came 2 practice English 2

quizás. that's maybe in Spanish, right?

sí. but what should i do??

maybe nothing?

what if he tries 2 kiss me?

follow your gut

it's as confused as my brain!

lol

but really mel if you're confused, don't do anything

that's probably good advice

good????

brilllllliant! :-)

don't worry, k?

k but what about 2night at suze's w/ miguel and justin both there??

sorry g2g my dad is calling ttyl

k bye

bye

Bye,
Mel

P.S. I feel a little better. I'm glad Cecily would never cut and paste or forward or print out our conversation. If Suze and I ever IMed like that, I bet Suze would show the whole world (or at least Cecily) the first chance she got. But Cecily is a good friend. I'm lucky she's my best friend!

If you're foolish enough to confide in Suze,
Your problema can get worse—— and become school news.

back home around ten
((we just dropped Miguel off))

Dear Diary,

Miguel and I met in Suze's lobby and went up to her party together in the elevator. It was a long ride and Miguel thought it was funny that the floors jumped from 12 to 14, skipping 13, simply because some people imagine that living on the 13th floor could bring bad luck. "Don't they realize the 14th floor *is* the 13th floor?" he asked.

Suze lives on the top floor, in a fancy penthouse with great views from the window.

We live on the second floor, which means no waits for the elevator but no views either. It also means we barely know our neighbors because we never make elevator chitchat.

Anyway, Suze let us in, and Miguel double-kissed her, and I could tell she liked that. A lot of kids from my class were standing around, and pizza arrived and everybody dived in. Suze gobbled two slices and let out a really loud burp, which was truly gross. (Miguel thought so too—I could tell.) I mean, we're not seven anymore! But Christopher burped back and said, "Aaahhh!" which was doubly gross. Maybe Suze and my *old* crush are meant for each other!

Suze asked Miguel if they have pizza in Spain. He said yes, but they eat it with a knife and fork. She said, "No offense, but I don't like spicy Spanish *tacos*."

Miguel smiled and said, "No offense, but Mexican food is spicy. Spanish food is not spicy. And in Spain, *taco* (Tah Coe) is not a food. It is what you call a 'curse word.'"

I felt like applauding! (hee, hee)

A girl named Ashley came up and introduced herself, saying, "*Hola, me llamo* (Oh La May Yom Oh) Ashley." She was sort of flirting, and at first I felt jealous, but I tried to remind myself that I don't own Miguel and he's not truly my bf anyway. She asked, "Is your name Michael in English?" He laughed and said, "I suppose so."

Suze must have seen me looking at them because she came over, motioned for me to step aside, then loudly whispered, "I heard about your sleepover with Miguel." She gave me a sicko smile that was really irritating.

I said, "It wasn't like that." Cecily might have told Suze about my plans with Miguel, but she would never have twisted things around or started a rumor.

"Mel, I'm not going to tell anyone."

"Suze, he's a friend of my whole family." She smirked as if she didn't believe me, so I added, "You think you know everything, but I think you should butt out of my business."

She arched one eyebrow. "You have a business? You're a businesswoman?"

I couldn't believe we were getting into a fight—at her party! But she was making me so so so mad! "I just mean: my friends are *my* business, not yours."

"What are you talking about?"

"Your attitude," I said. My heart was hammering inside me. "You've been trying to steal Cecily, and you asked Justin if he liked me, and now you're assuming stuff about Miguel." Even though I was upset, I was still trying to speak quietly, which was more than I can say for Suze. Instead of whispering, she was talking in her regular voice. I wished she had a volume knob that I could turn down—or off!

"Trying to *steal* Cecily?! First of all, she's a person not a thing, so she's not stealable. Second, she's allowed to have friends besides you. Third—wait, why am I even defending myself? You're the one who always acts like you have better things to do than to talk to me. Which is fine. It's a free country. But still, *your* attitude can be annoying, you know."

"What are *you* talking about?" I definitely hadn't expected her to call *me* annoying.

"You're always avoiding me. I invite you to a party, and you make it seem like you're doing me this huge favor just showing up. I'm not a horrible person."

"I never said you were a horrible person." (Not to her face anyway!)

"You act like you think it."

I had no clue what to say, so I just poured myself some juice.

"Look," Suze continued, "I moved here and I didn't

know anybody. Our class is pretty small, and some of the nicest kids were already your friends. That doesn't mean I was trying to take them away from you. Everything is not about you, you know."

Now I was truly speechless. Or in shock or something.

"Really, Melanie," she continued, "I'm nice to you! If I didn't like you, I would not have invited you tonight. And I would have asked Justin out *without* asking you first. Remember?"

I should have said: "How could I forget?" Or: "You didn't ask me thoughtfully. You asked me trickily!" Instead, I mumbled, "I guess."

She made a face as if to say, "See!"

I asked, "So did you ask him out?"

She lowered her voice—finally. "Yeah. He said no. But he's supposed to come tonight—on the late side. I bet he will show up because I told him you'd be here." My heart did a flip-flop and I hoped she couldn't tell. "I still think he likes you."

"Really? Why? Did he say anything?" I couldn't believe Suze had somehow gotten me to change the subject from her meanness to Justin's niceness.

"I just think so." Suze leaned forward, glanced at Miguel, and said, "Even though you said you didn't like Justin, I think you do and don't want to admit it, not even to yourself. No offense. I mean, you know you better than I know you."

It was the kind of oozy comment that would usually drive me insane, but this time it didn't. Because I knew she had a tiny point.

"Have you heard from Cecily?" I asked.

"No. She gets back in three days," Suze said. "Maybe we can all go shopping."

"Maybe." But I knew I wasn't going to be the one to call her. The doorbell rang, and Suze flounced off to let more people in.

I wasn't sure if I'd actually want to go shopping with Cecily and Suze, but I did like feeling included. And I figured maybe I could tryyyy to appreciate Suze's okay side. She must have one or Cecily wouldn't like her, right?

Someday I may shop with Suze,
but friendship might work best in twos!

230

Well, since I'd thought the party would be more awkward than fun, I'd asked Mom to pick us up early—at 8:30. Of course I didn't know Justin would be arriving late!

I found Miguel and told him we had to go. He double-kissed all the girls and they ate it up, especially Ashley, who said, "*Adiós*, Michael," and giggled. I thanked Suze and she said, "I'll call you."

I said, "Okay," which felt weird. Then we left and she closed the door behind us.

In the hallway, Miguel said, "That was a fun *fiesta*," and I agreed. I was half disappointed not to have seen Justin, but half relieved that Justin and Miguel hadn't met.

We were in front of the elevators, and I pressed the down button. The doors popped open and guess who walked out? Justin!!

"Bad timing!" I said.

"No. Just-in-time Justin timing!"

His eyes were smiling, and mine smiled back, but I didn't want to smile too much with Miguel right there.

Justin got out of the elevator and Miguel got in, but that seemed abrupt, so I said, "Wait, Miguel. Come out. I want you to meet Justin."

Miguel came out and extended his hand—which Justin was not expecting. "Hello. I am Miguel."

"Miguel!" Justin said, and shook his hand. "Suze said you'd be here: The Boyfriend from Barcelona."

"Valencia," Miguel corrected, though neither of us commented on the other B word. I could, however, feel myself getting pinker by the second.

"Melanie told our whole class about Spain," Justin said. "The bonfires and the bullfight."

Guess whose mouth once again stopped working?

"Perhaps you will visit my country someday," Miguel said.

"Perhaps," Justin said, and smiled at me because kids don't usually say the word "perhaps."

I just stood there, quiet as MouseMouse.

Then Christopher came out of Suze's apartment and joined us in the narrow hallway. He asked Miguel what he liked best about New York. Miguel said, "Above the ground, the skyscrapers. Beneath the ground, the subway." He described riding in the front subway car and looking into the huge black tunnel.

Funny. Tonight's party and our subway ride were the

only truly unplanned parts of Miguel's whole trip. And he loved them. I'd always thought of the subway as a way to get somewhere, not an amazing experience.

Miguel was describing everything we saw underground and said, "It was stupen— No, it was awesome! It was cool!"

Everyone laughed.

"Did Mel's family take you to a Mets game?" Christopher asked, and he and Miguel started discussing *béisbol*.

I took a step toward Justin and finally got my mouth to work, but barely. You won't believe what it said. This is what it said: "Suze mentioned that you have a girlfriend too." I don't know what made it say that! It was worse than standing there mute.

"Girlfriend?"

"From camp?"

He looked at me like I was crazy, so I mumbled, "Never mind," and tried to become invisible. Which didn't work.

I wish wish wished I had just gone down in the elevator that Justin came up in!

"Oh! Wait! I know what you mean!" he finally said.

"I told Suze I had a special friend at camp who is a girl. And I do. My sister!"

"Your sister?" I didn't want Justin or Miguel to be able to read my face.

"My sister, Katie." Justin leaned toward me. "Suze is okay, but you know how loud she can be. I didn't think it was any of her business if I did or didn't have a girlfriend."

Another elevator came and Christopher got in. "C'mon, Melanie. C'mon, Miguel."

We got in, and I called out to Justin, "Have a great rest-of-the-summer."

"Maybe I'll see you," he said.

I didn't answer. But inside I smiled.

Happily,
Melanie Martin
Party Girl

Dear Diary,   Same night, elevenish

"I'm going to the corner," Mom said. "We're out of milk." Mom and Dad like milk in their morning coffee.

"Can I come?"

"It's pretty late."

"It's summer."

"Okay, let's go."

On the corner, we saw a man with a scraggly beard and a shopping cart full of books, plastic bags, empty cans, and blankets. He was wearing too many clothes for a warm night, but Mom said he doesn't have a home (or closet) to put them in. She said homelessness is a problem that can't be easily fixed but that when I'm older, I can volunteer at a soup kitchen in our neighborhood. I watched as the man searched inside a garbage can and found part of a sandwich that someone else had thrown away. Since we were buying food, Mom bought him a bagel and an apple. He said, "God bless you."

I don't think I can write a poem
about a man who has no home.
He searched for food in a garbage can;
he has no money, but he's still a man.

New York has millions of people in it, not even

counting all the tourists. And some of them are a lot less lucky than others.

Sadly,

M.

Sunday June 24

1:30 at home 🏢

Dear Diary,

This morning Uncle Angel wanted to go to church in Harlem.

"Church?" Matt said, because it's not like we usually go to church.

"Harlem?" I said, because it's not like we usually go to Harlem.

"Do we have to?" we both asked Mom and Dad, and they said yes, because it was Miguel and Angel's last day here. Mom even started singing a jazz song called "Take the A Train."

We got up early and met Uncle Angel and Miguel and went up to West 138th Street to hear a gospel service at the most famous church in Harlem, the Abyssinian Baptist Church. According to Uncle Angel's guidebook, the ABC was founded in 1808.

His book says a lot about Harlem. How Duke Ellington and Ella Fitzgerald and Louis Armstrong made music, and Langston Hughes wrote poems, and Fidel Castro and the Beatles visited, and Bill Clinton has an office there.

I realize race and religion are both touchy subjects, but if I can't be honest in my own diary, where can I be honest?

So here goes: Where I live, there are more white people than black people. In Harlem, there are more black people than white people. *We* were the minority!

Actually, I don't know why I'm even writing "white" and "black." We're all different shades of beige and brown. No one's white or black. Miguel and Uncle Angel have been amazed at how if you look around New York, you see all different colors of skin and hair and eyes. You hear lots of Spanish too!

As for religion, in school we're always learning about people who believe in God but who, next thing you know, start a big war with people who believe in God in a different way.

Well, I'm not completely sure what I believe. But I don't think God would want people to be constantly fighting over Him (or Her).

I also hope that He—or She—wouldn't mind that on most Sunday mornings, I'm in bed fast asleep.

Today at 9:00 A.M., we were in the ABC. It was packed! It is a very popular church. And welcoming. A man held open the red door for us, and a lady wearing a white dress and white gloves ushered us in, and a man next to me shared his open songbook when everyone started singing.

The singing was beautiful! Organ music filled the room, and dozens of men and women wearing flowing crimson robes were standing and swaying and clapping in the choir loft above the preacher. Their voices were so rich and spirited it made me want to sing along!

The preacher had a great voice too. Dad said he was the Reverend Dr. Calvin O. Butts III. I could tell that Matt was dying to make a joke. For once, though, he didn't. Which made me kind of proud of Little DumDum.

Dr. Butts stood in front of the big stained-glass windows and said nobody's perfect but everyone can try to be inclusive even if you once felt excluded. He said the church is a community and a home where everyone can belong. "The doors of the church are always open. If you are a visitor and this is your first time here, we are glad you came and please stand up."

Matt hopped up! Mom, Dad, Angel, and Miguel did too! If I'd had a sign that said I DON'T KNOW THESE PEOPLE, I would have held it, but I didn't. And since everyone was looking anyway, I realized I had to stand up. So I did.

The lady in front of me, an older black woman with a pretty pink hat, turned and said "Welcome," and held out her right hand for me to shake. A man behind me smiled with dark eyes and extended his hand. So did the man next to me. And another lady in front of me. Everyone was shaking my hand and smiling kindly and welcoming me, and suddenly it wasn't embarrassing, it was sort of warm and comforting.

To tell you the truth, I'd walked into the church

feeling a tiny bit alone, maybe because it's Miguel's last day here. But after the reverend talked about us all as brothers and sisters and family and everyone shook my hand, well, I felt less alone. More like smothered, but in a good way. Like a pork chop in apple sauce!

The reverend was also saying that everyone has a gift and that we can be generous and give what we can to help others in need. People started saying "Amen" and "That's right." Even the people up in the back balconies.

"You have to figure out what you have to offer," Dr. Butts continued. "Some of you may have the gift of time. Or the gift of singing. Or the gift of cooking. Or the gift of writing."

Writing?!

Was he talking to me? Do I have the gift of writing? And if so, am I supposed to figure out how to be generous with that gift?

Maybe. Maybe I'm not supposed to just send IMs and e-mails and worry about them. Maybe I'm supposed to realize the world isn't only me and my friends. It's huge. In fact, there are whole worlds I didn't even know of right here in Manhattan!

240

I bet I'll always obsess about friends and boys. But maybe I can obsess a teensy weensy bit less. And instead of getting so upset, maybe I can keep trying to remember how lucky I am.

"God has smiled on me," the chorus started singing. "God's been good to me." I listened and reminded myself that I've been very fortunate, even though I sometimes forget.

For instance, I'm not homeless. Some people don't have a family who cares about them, but I definitely do. When Mom and Dad take us places, or even when they just make pancakes or drop us off and pick us up, those are grown-up ways of showing love.

And many of the grown-ups in the pews today probably have never been to Europe, but I've even been to Haarlem, the pretty town in Holland that gave our Harlem its name.

Soon it was time for the offering. A brass bowl got passed around so people could put in money for the church and for sick or hungry people. I was sitting between Dad and Mom, and Dad reached into his pocket and put a ten-dollar bill in the shiny bowl. He was about to pass it directly to Mom.

"Wait," I whispered, and dug deep down inside my pocket. I pulled out three crinkled-up dollar bills (which was all I had) and added it to the little pile of money.

Mom nodded at me, and Dad put his arm around me and gave my shoulder a squeeze. You know what? It felt good. And Dad's arm didn't make me nervous or anxious or jumpy at all.

After church, we went out for a farewell lunch at Sylvia's. We ate delicious ribs, beans, crunchy fried chicken, corn bread, corn on the cob, and sweet potato pie. (Miguel also liked the collard greens—yuk!) And we got to meet Sylvia! She's as nice as can be, but she's only my height, which, for a grown-up, is *short*!

We also stopped by the Apollo Theater. It is a landmark, which means it can get fixed up but not torn down. Inside we saw pictures of musicians who have performed there: Stevie Wonder, Miles Davis, Dizzy Gillespie, Aretha Franklin, Nat King Cole, and Frankie Lyman. Mom started singing "Unforgettable," so I gave her a poke, but then Dad started singing, "Why do fools fall in love?" and I had to poke him too.

Finally, we walked along a historic street called

Striver's Row. It is on West 139th Street between Frederick Douglass and Adam Clayton Powell Jr. boulevards. Mom and Dad wanted Uncle Angel and Miguel to see Striver's Row because the red brick houses were built in 1890 and it's in Uncle Angel's guidebook.

"Why is it called Striver's Row?" Matt asked.

"Because striving is what it's all about," Dad said. "Working hard and doing your best. It's not Achiever's Row or Got Rich Row. Life isn't just about getting but *reaching* and growing. Giving your all and giving back."

Wow. Had the sermon inspired Dad too?

I guess we can all work harder and aim higher and think bigger.

I'll probably sleep in next Sunday, but I'm glad I went to church and to Harlem today.

P.S. Uncle Angel and Miguel are doing last-minute shopping, and we're about to drive them to the airport. Matt just finished making the pretend pack of cigarettes.

In the CAR coming home from JFK

Dear Diary,

It was a close one!

On the way to JFK, Mom wanted to stop at the Queens Museum of Art to see the Panorama of the City of New York. Dad said that was crazy. Mom said it was not. Dad said that you have to get to the airport early for international flights, and there was no more time for tourism. Mom pleaded. Dad gave in—but grouchily.

Well, the Panorama is a huge huge huge scale model of all five boroughs. It was originally built for a world's fair. It's like a mini New York, with lights that go on and off. We circled it and pointed out everything we'd visited.

Draped over the World Trade Center is a red-white-and-blue ribbon laced in a loose figure eight, probably because the idea of removing the twin towers was too sad or *triste* (Tree Stay). But everything changes—especially cities—and someday there may be a model of the Freedom Tower.

After twenty minutes, Dad announced, "Miranda, you and the kids can do whatever you like, but I'm taking Miguel and Angel to the airport right now."

"Me too!" I said and we all followed Dad down a gigundous elevator and walked outside to see the shining steel Unisphere, the largest globe in the world.

Uncle Angel lit a cigarette and Matt rushed over and gave him the fake pack. He said, "I made these because real cigarettes are bad for you." Miguel translated, and at first Uncle Angel looked confused, but then he looked half amused, half touched. He even gave Matt double cheek kisses, which Matt did *not* expect.

"That's where you guys are going," Matt said, pointing to Spain on the Unisphere.

"Not if we don't leave ASAP!" Dad said.

"What means ASAP?" Uncle Angel asked.

I said, "As Soon As Possible."

Well, the traffic to JFK, which had been fine, turned terrible, and Dad was cranky and cursed twice and even muttered, "You should have listened, Miranda!"

The only funny part of the car ride was when Matt sneezed and Uncle Angel asked if he was constipated. Matt repeated, "Constipated??" and Mom explained to us that *constipado* (Cone Stee Pa Dough) means to be stuffed-up or have a cold. Even Dad laughed a little, but then went back to being mad at every single other car on the highway.

Somehow we made it to the airport and parked. Dad and Uncle Angel strode ahead, Mom followed holding Matt's hand, and Miguel and I were last. We were all walking as fast as we could, and we accompanied Uncle Angel and Miguel as far as we were allowed. At the last *minuto* I said, "Miguel?"

"*¿Sí, señorita?*"

Deep down, I think we both knew that we liked each other but that it could be ages before we'd see each other again. We were almost out of time, so I just plain blurted out, "Is it going to be hard to stay close when we are far apart?"

"May Lah Nee, we can always be friends. Special friends, true?"

"True. Forever friends."

"*Amigos para siempre* (Ah Me Gose Pa Ra Syem Pray). And we will see each other again someday. Don't you think?"

"*Sí.*" I looked up into his chocolate eyes.

Suddenly, even though I hadn't planned it, and even

though I had to go on tiptoe, I kissed him—right on the forehead! It was not the kiss I had been imagining. But I liked it. I did. It was a quick kiss and I didn't close my eyes; I kept them open so I could see his smile.

For me, the kiss was partly a handshake agreement. I wanted to seal the deal that we would stay friends forever. I don't know if our love was real, but I want our friendship to be.

For me, the kiss was also partly a goodbye kiss. In some ways, I knew we were setting each other free. He would always be welcome in my home, but I wasn't going to carry a torch to light the way anymore.

We caught up to Matt and the grown-ups and I said, "I hope things work out with your dad and mom."

"*Gracias.*"

"What if they don't?" I asked, then immediately wished I hadn't.

"I don't know, May Lah Nee. I wish it could be the way it was. But if they remain separate, then at least I still have a mother and a father."

Next thing you know, Mom, Dad, Matt, and I were waving *adiós adiós adiós* to Miguel and Uncle Angel as they hurried toward their gate. Matt and I kept waving and waving long after the grown-ups stopped. Miguel was waving too. We three kept waving until Miguel finally disappeared—until he was just a dot in the universe.

I took a deep breath, turned around, then we four M's walked back through the airport toward our car.

"Whoa! Check it out!" Matt pointed up at a dozen silvery helium balloons floating on the ceiling of the airport terminal. One said "We'll miss you"; one said "Welcome"; one said "I love you"; one said "Bon voyage."

They were all mixed up, which is how I feel a lot too.

Forever yours, Mixed⋄Up Melanie

P.S. In the car ride back, Mom said nice things about Miguel and Angel, and Dad did too, but he also said, "Having guests is a lot of work." Mom and I gave each other a little look because, after all, our apartment is about to be full of more guests for Dad's surprise party.

P.P.S.

I think Miguel will stay my friend.
I hope our story will not end.

in a WEirdmood

Dear Diary,

When you read a book, the author has figured everything out for you.

But when you write a diary—or live your life—you have to figure it out for yourself. It's like *you* are the author.

So allow me to introduce myselves: Melanie, Melanie, Melanie.

Lately I've been thinking about how many me's there are. We all have so many selves and sides!

I'm a daughter, sister, best friend, regular friend, almost sixth grader, sort of ex-girlfriend, sort of ex-enemy, traveler, diary keeper, New Yorker, and former mice owner.

If you noticed that I said "former mice owner," it's because Mom said the mice always smell terrible, and Dad said, "Dogs are good because they say, 'Let's go for a walk,' and cats are good because they say, 'Relax! Read a book!' but mice just make more mice."

Somehow we knew we couldn't keep them all anymore. Even Matt knew.

Not that he and I didn't protest about it!

Well, Suze called, and I told her about our mice is-sues, and she said her aunt is a science teacher and could maybe take them. Then she called her aunt, and the aunt said she could give some to her summer stu-dents as pets, and she could keep the others to use in her classroom for experiments, but she assured us, "not mean experiments."

So yesterday we gave them to her. All zillion of them.

Except MouseMouse, which Matt gets to keep. And his (or her) brother (or sister) Ahoy, which Matt gave to Lily.

Mom said maybe we can get another pet sometime, but just one, not a pair. She also said change is good. Which might be true.

Mulling things Over,
Melanie (BUT WHICH ONE?)

Dear Diary,

Matt and I played Boggle today. Here's how he thought "kissed" was spelled: KIST. I made fun of him, so he kept crossing his eyes because he knows I can't stand that.

Since Dad is at work, Mom and I and even Matt have been getting ready for the party. We've cooked, baked, bought wine (a.k.a. Love Potion!), ordered a king-size cake, and hidden things in the neighbor's freezer. Matt and I even worked on a toast.

He asked me, "Does everyone have a midlife crisis?"

"I don't think so."

"How long do they last?"

"How should I know?"

Mom asked me to help her finish the Hopper puzzle since it's almost almost almost done.

She and I were finding puzzle pieces and talking about all the friends and relatives who are coming to surprise Dad. Poor Dad still seems so bummed about turning forty this weekend that it's tempting to tell him about the secret celebration. But I never would!

Mom said, "I see you took off your necklace."

"I did. I might put it back on for Dad's party. I'm just not going to wear it all the time."

"That makes sense."

"I was thinking of buying myself a necklace with my allowance money. A little apple from the Big Apple."

"Nice idea." Mom nodded. "And Lambie, I hope you know that you and Miguel gave each other bigger gifts than that necklace."

"What do you mean?"

"You gave each other an inside view of another country. If I could give my students field trips like that, I could enrich their lives!"

"Cecily loves your field trips."

Mom smiled, then added, "And also, Mel, a first kiss is not nothing." I thought two things. 1. Moms remember everything, and 2. That was a double negative, so she meant, "A first kiss *is* something."

It is. I'm glad mine was with Miguel.

The puzzle was almost done, and I was trying to connect two pieces that looked like they belonged together, but I couldn't force them. Then I picked up a piece in front of me and it clicked right in.

"Love is hard for grown-ups too," Mom said. "Oh, but guess what? Miguel's dad, Antonio, phoned this morning while you were asleep. He called to thank us and to say that Miguel really liked New York. And also to say that he and his wife have moved back in together."

"That's great!"

"It is. It's lucky when people can work things out."

Looking down at the puzzle, I mumbled, "You know, at first I liked Miguel so much that I wanted everything to work out and nothing to change."

"I know," Mom said. "But everything does change. Your own dad is struggling with this. He'd like to stay in his thirties, but he can't. Saturday's his big birthday, ready or not."

"We'll be ready. We'll make it fun for him."

"We will. And he'll like his forties and fifties." Mom leaned forward. "And someday, Mel, you'll like your second real kiss—which will be your first kiss with someone else."

I said, "Mom!!!" but did not add, "How do you know there hasn't already been a second kiss?"

"You don't think I was ever eleven or twelve or a teenager?"

"Were you?"

"Careful, Cutie, or I won't let you put in the last piece." She handed over the prized last piece. It was an elbow—a funny bone. It belonged to the woman in the diner with two men and one waiter. None of them is talking. The painting is called *Nighthawks.*

"Nighthawks are birds, right?" I said. "But look—these people are trapped. There's not even a door for going in or going out."

"Huh. I'd never looked at it that way."

"Maybe I'll be an art teacher someday."

"You could be anything you want," Mom said.

Dear Diary,

Cecily's back, so she came over this morning and we had everything bagels with nothing on them. And I told her everything and left nothing out. I even said that one of the best things about Miguel's visit ended up being that I got to know New York City better.

Not that I need Miguel to enjoy my hometown. I can do that alone. Or with my family. Or with my best friend, Cecily.

> New York is full of places,
> of sights and sounds and faces,
> and I, Melanie the Poet,
> will never fully know it.

I asked Cecily about *her* week with her dad. She said they went to Sea World. Then her cell phone rang and it was Suze. Cecily asked, "Okay if she comes over?" I shrugged. Cecily told her to join us and after they hung up, Cecily said in a nice way, "Melanie, you have new friends and I don't mind."

"Who?"

"Justin!" She smiled, so I did too. Then Suze came over, and suddenly the three of us were on my sofa watching TV. At least Matt was upstairs at Lily's!

Mom looked at us and must have done the math— one, two, three—because she said, "I have to run an errand midtown. Want to come?"

"Sure," Cecily called out.

Suze whispered, "An errand??"

Cecily whispered back, "It won't be boring."

I appreciated Cecily's defending my mom, and I thought someone should tell Suze that she's a loud whisperer.

Well, Mom got what she needed at the gift shop of the American Folk Art Museum on West 53rd Street, then asked if we wanted to "whirl through." Cecily was willing, Suze was reluctant, and I said I'd already seen the Statue of Liberty weather vane. Mom said, "How about MoMA?"

I said, "No Ma."

She laughed. "Then, girls, let's cross the street and I'll show you what's in the Donnell Library."

"She wants us to look at books?" Suze whispered.

"I want you to look at Winnie-the-Pooh," Mom said, not even covering up that she'd overheard.

"The movie?" Suze asked.

"The teddy. The real Winnie-the-Pooh," Mom said.

"There *is* a real Winnie-the-Pooh?" Cecily asked.

"He lives right over there on the second floor," Mom said, pointing. Suze sighed, but Cecily and I were excited, and we all followed Mom into the library and took the elevator to the second floor.

Remember when I told you I came face to face with the Statue of Liberty? Well, we all came face to face with Winnie-the-Pooh!! And Kanga, Eeyore, Tigger, and Piglet!! The real live actual childhood stuffed animals of A. A. Milne's son, Christopher!!!

Cecily's mouth flopped open. "Do people know they're here? You'd think this place would be mobbed!"

"It's not a secret," Mom said, "but it's not in all the guidebooks either. New York is such a smorgasbord."

"Smorgaswhat?" Cecily asked.

"The city is like a big banquet, a feast. There are so many temptations you can't sample them all."

"No offense, Mrs. Martin," Suze said, "but I don't see

what's so great about a bunch of old stuffies behind glass. I mean, who cares?"

I looked at the animals again, and it was as if Suze had just poisoned them:

Winnie-the-Pooh seemed worn and small, and his friends looked tired, one and all.

But then I thought that I shouldn't keep giving Suze the power to ruin things for me. I had to make myself immune to her Poison Potion.

"Who cares?!" Cecily stared at Suze. "I care! Suze, this is the REAL Winnie-the-Pooh! Read this caption. It says Winnie was given to Christopher Robin for his first birthday. These aren't Disney Store stuffies. This is The Original Winnie!!"

Mom smiled. "I care too. This little teddy and his friends are footnotes to literary history. Even Teddy Roosevelt liked teddy bears. And as presidents go, he was *mucho* macho."

"Look at poor Winnie's stitched-up paw," I said. "Can't you just see Christopher Robin holding it and dragging Winnie downstairs headfirst, bump bump bump?"

Suze leaned in more closely and, to her credit, said, "I guess I can kind of picture that." I gave her a tiny smile.

We walked up Avenue of the Americas, and for a minute, it was Suze and Mom ahead, and Cecily and me behind.

"Does Suze know about Snow Bear?" I asked.

"Omigod. You kidding? No way! And don't you tell her!"

"Never!! Your secrets are safe with me if mine are safe with you."

"Deal," she said. "Forever and for always."

We quietly low-fived each other.

Safely yours,
The Original Melanie

almost bedtime ©

Dear Diary,

Matt just came in and said, "Knock, knock."

"No."

"No?!"

"No."

"You can't say no. You have to say 'Who's there?'"

"I can say no if I want."

"C'mon, say 'Who's there?'"

I sighed. "Fine. Who's there?"

"Winnie."

"Winnie who?"

"It's NOT 'Winnie who'! It's Winnie-the-Pooh!!"

"Ha ha ha."

"I have another: What did Winnie-the-Pooh say when he was offered dessert?"

"What?"

"No, thanks, I'm stuffed!"

"Matt, are you done yet?"

"Yeah, but wanna play New York City Monopoly?"

I said sure, because sometimes I like to surprise us both and be a Perfect Big Sister.

Playfully,
Melanie the P.B.S.

Dear Diary,

Dad's party was fun even though it was all grown-ups. Everyone yelled "Surprise" and sang "Happy Birthday," and I could tell Dad loved having his friends over. I think he'd forgotten how many friends he has. He also loved that it was a surprise.

One of his childhood friends made a toast. He had a cleft chin, or as Matt whispered to me, a butt chin. The man said that when Dad and he were campers together, Dad always insisted on the bottom bunk, not the top bunk, because then he could run around and raise h-ll and, when the counselor returned, Dad could jump back in bed real quick.

Believe it or not, that was not hard to picture.

Matt and I made a toast too. We recited:

You've been a grouch and you think you're old,
    but you are young and your heart is gold!

Then we gave Dad a cardboard heart that we'd

261

spray painted gold and decorated. He pinned it on his shirt, and everyone clapped.

Anyway, after the party but before bed, Dad and I snuck back into the kitchen in our pajamas for milk and leftover cake.

"So what about you, Melanie? Did you have a nice time?"

"Tonight? Yes!"

"How about during Miguel's trip?"

The question seemed out of the blue, but I said, "I think he enjoyed it."

"And you?"

I stayed quiet, and Dad did too, and silence probably worked better than if Dad had started prying, because next thing you know, I was talking and talking.

"I liked seeing Miguel and doing all the New York stuff. But you know how you weren't looking forward to your birthday and then it turned out fun? Well, I was looking so so so forward to Miguel's trip that his visit couldn't possibly live up to my expectations—is that the right word?"

"Yes." Dad smiled.

"Things didn't feel as perfect as they did in Spain. But I think I've seen too many movies, and I was being dumb because I imagined that a boy and a girl who like each other always just keep liking each other more and more."

"Oh, Melleroo, nothing and no one is perfect, but don't go giving up on love! You're eleven. Boys will soon be lining up around the block, and I'll be beating them back with a stick. Or maybe with"—Dad imitated a Spanish accent—"a *béisbol* bat."

"That's horrible, Dad! I wouldn't want you to hit anybody. Especially somebody who liked me!"

"It *is* horrible. I don't know why I said it. It's one of those things fathers are programmed to say to their lovely daughters."

"Am I a lovely daughter?"

"Honey Bun, some guy is going to be so lucky to have you that it'll be hard for me not to be jealous. Is that horrible too? Fatherhood isn't easy for us old men."

"You're not old. It's true that you like old-fogey operas, but sometimes you and Matt are peas in a pod."

"Really?" Dad looked happy.

"Dad, hate to break it to you, but that is *not* a compliment. Unless you like being immature."

"Beats geezerhood."

"Dad, don't worry. You're forty years young."

"My, my, look who's telling who not to worry."

"Whom!"

Dad laughed. "Melanie, when I was a boy, back when dinosaurs prowled the earth, I liked girls like you. The smart, sweet, funny ones got me right here." He poked himself in the heart.

I could have said, "The boys in our grade like popular

girls with big chests," but instead I said, "You're still a boy. A big boy. A B.B."

"I thought I was a Big Pig. A B.P.?" He took his fork and stole a bite of my cake since he'd already finished his.

"Hey!"

"I'm a B.B. and a B.P. And I'm forty! It *is* a shocker. I even have some gray hair."

"Not much. And Mom likes it. She calls it *silver*."

"Silver." He nodded. "Your mother's a keeper. She looked so pretty tonight."

"Dad, I'm going to ask you something and don't make a face, okay? Is Miguel the kind of guy I *should* carry a torch for? Do you think he's a keeper?"

Dad smiled. "Keep him as a friend. Who knows, maybe you two will meet again when you're older. But honey, he was the first of many. You've got lots of guys in your future. And I've got lots of sticks."

"Dad!"

"Let me tell you something else, Kiddo."

"What?"

"I'm always here for you. You know what unconditional love is?"

"Not really."

"It's love no-matter-what. And that's how Mom and I love you and Matt. We love you even when you ruin laundry or misplace mouse babies or spill milk or get bad grades or anything."

"I don't get bad grades."

"What I mean is, boyfriends come and go, but Dad Love lasts forever. You're stuck with me. So when you're worrying about boys, I want you to know that I'm right here. I'm always here."

"You're a little weird, Dad," I said, because I was too embarrassed to say, "I unconditionally love you too."

Here's what I did do: I stuck a candle on what was left of my piece of cake and struck a match (something I'd just learned how to do) and lit the candle and pushed my plate toward Dad and sang, "Happy Birthnight to You, Happy Birthnight to You, Happy Birthnight Dear Daaaaaaaaaad, Happy Birthnight to You!"

Dad beamed. "I've been around four decades, and no one's ever wished me a happy birthnight."

"Then it's about time!"

Dad mussed my hair. "Cupcake, you're a keeper too."

Since it was fun giving Miguel that surprise airport kiss, I got up, walked over to Dad, and gave him a peck on the cheek. Not a Spanish *beso beso*, just a daughter-father kiss.

He didn't say anything. But he smiled like a little boy.

With unconditional Love,
Melanie

July 1
1:00 P.M.

Dear Diary,

I went online, and justjustin IMed me.

He wrote: **sup mialene**

I wrote: nm jstuin

u ok

yes. u?

your amigo still there?

he left

oh. how many mice do u have now?

`one.`

`raelly? ur kddiing?`

I was thinking how fun it is to get and send IMs! It's like passing notes. And I was about to explain about the mice when the phone rang. It was Justin! He said, "I figured I'd call instead of wearing out our fingers. So what happened to the millions of mice?"

I told him, and he laughed but listened too, then told me that he'd gone kayaking with his sister and they almost got stuck in a thunderstorm.

He's really easy to talk to.

He said, "Hey, we have an extra ticket to go to a musical because my dad can't come. Want to go? My mom and sister and I would have to pick you up in about forty-five minutes."

"Let me find out." I asked, and Mom said yes. I think she likes that Justin's mom is also a teacher (of math, not art).

I said, "I can go! I'm free."

"Good, because I barely saw you at Suze's."

"Did you have fun at her party?"

"It was okay, but Suze is Suze, you know what I mean?"

I laughed because I knew exactly exactly exactly what he meant. "Well, it was nice of you to call."

"I'm a nice guy."

I laughed again. "Listen, we better hang up so I can get ready."

"Okay," he said, but he didn't hang up, so I didn't either. And then we both did.

Some relationships happen fast, but I guess it's good when they build slowly. After all, we're not mice that become great-great-grandparents in two seconds! We're people, and even though some say "Life is short," I think it's long if you're eleven.

> I want to grow up; it is true.
> But I don't want to just rush through.
> It's better to enjoy the here and now.
> Am I sort of learning how?

I *am* learning that nothing stays the same. And that that's okay. But I want to be careful with my heart because I don't want to get it all bruised up again. I mean, I just got my balance back!

From now on, I'm not going to go Sooooooooo crazy about boys and stuff.

Then again, I don't want to be toooooo careful either, because hearts *are* for sharing. And feeling. Plus it's fun when a guy you like likes you back!

I wonder if today will feel like a date. A *teenage* date—but with chaperones. Mom walked in with folded pants, tops, and bras. I asked, "Do you think I'll be impossible when I'm a teenager?"

"Impossible?" She laughed. "No, honey, I think you'll always be possible."

"Really?"

"Not all teens are terrors. I should know. I teach them."

"But some are?"

"Well, sure. Just as some kids are."

Matt the Brat burst in hopping on one foot. "What has three legs and barks?" I stared at him. "A three-legged dog!" He continued, "What has two legs and barks?"

"What?"

"A weird kid!!" He barked twice and hopped away.

"Mom, hate to tell you, but you have a very weird son."

She didn't disagree, just asked what musical we're seeing.

"*Wonderful Town*."

"That's great! New York *is* a wonderful town!"

It's true. Some people say, "New York is a nice place to visit but I wouldn't want to live there." Well, I live here and I love it! In fact, it's almost as if I've been writing a whole travel diary about it! Instead of a Melanie Abroad diary, this really was a Melanie At Home diary!

And even though my brother can be pretty dorky, I guess I'm realizing that deep down I love my whole family—and whole city.

I even love myself. Loving yourself is extra smart because you're always there.

There's no place like home and there's no one like me;
I love my family, my friends, and N.Y.C.!

Of course, I still love traveling too! But even when we're *not* going anywhere, we're all traveling in our own lives.

271

We're not stuck or trapped like the Statue of Liberty or that Goya boy or those puzzle people or even Winnie-the-Pooh. We're alive!

I mean, think about it. The Statue of Liberty is cool, but no one ever gives *her* a necklace or invites *her* to a matinee!

Then again, she probably appreciates what's right in front of her four-and-a-half-foot nose: all of New York City!

Well, I better stop writing and start changing. The world is waiting, and I have a date!!! (Sort of.)

With Love Love Love
from Manhattan,

Melanie Martin
City Girl

I'M SO SO SO GRATEFUL TO:

Family

Emme, Elizabeth, and Robert Ackerman: wonderful travelers and ruthless editors. *Os quiero un montón.*

My mom, Marybeth Weston Lobdell; stepniece, Olivia Lobdell; and brother, Mark Weston, for their suggestions and encouragements.

My mom-in-law, Gene Ackerman, for knowing gorillas from monkeys.

All the Squam Lake Cousins, especially Andy Bird, Matt Bird, Stephanie May, Sarah Jeffrey, and nephew Felix Ackerman, owner of The Original DogDog.

Nephew David Weston for letting me steal his jokes.

Matty Reategui for everything always.

And Cousin Bonnie Landes Beer for her insightful comments and for sharing the story of her sweet little bird who made the mistake of flying into a dishwasher. (R.I.P. Sparky!)

Friends

Maureen Davison, Patty Dann, and Cathy Roos, who read all my pages and made me reach higher and dig deeper. Your friendship is such a gift.

Vanessa Wilcox, who took me (and therefore Mel) to the ABC; Ann Johnson for lunch at Sylvia's; and Bascove and Michael for the Bargemusic.

Tom Klingenstein, for being an expert on the Empire State Building.

The inspiring and enthusiastic students at Trinity, North Street, Friends, Colonial, CSG, Spence, and other schools.

Our many Spanish friends, including Javier Muñoz-Basols and Nuria Martín.

Julia Black and omg, owg! (That's you, Livi!)

Pros

I thank my lucky ☆ Stars (estrellas or STray Yoss) for
Knopf's dazzling Michelle Frey, Michele Burke,
Sarah Hokanson,* Marci Roth, Ericka O'Rourke,
Nancy Hinkel, Joan Slattery, Alison Kolani, and
Shanta-Small-Who's-Rather-Tall.
Let's hear it too for Curtis Brown's fabulous
Laura Peterson, Ed Wintle, and Dave Barbor!

And now a final rhyme:
A GREAT big hurray
to Caroline Rhea!

Carol Weston is the author of *The Diary of Melanie Martin*, *Melanie Martin Goes Dutch*, and *With Love from Spain, Melanie Martin*. She is the well-known advice columnist of *Girls' Life* magazine and the author of *For Girls Only, For Teens Only, Private and Personal*, and *Girltalk: All the Stuff Your Sister Never Told You*. Carol met her husband in Spain, and they live in Manhattan with two daughters, one cat, one bunny, and one hamster. Visit www.melaniemartin.com.